"What happened to me that winter still keeps me up at night. It was the sort of thing no one should ever have to go through. Jan turned out to be a bigger foreigner than I'd ever imagined. My oldest friend, Kyle, became someone I hardly knew. My neighbor Christian unexpectedly left New York. And me? You'd think this mess I'm about to lay out would've opened my eyes. I guess it did. But not in the cathartic way you read about in self-help books. At least I've been cured of my thing for foreign men—well, almost. Now, I'm involved with an American. Still, he's a cop, and that's foreign enough for me."

the foreigner

the foreigner

meg castaldo

POCKET
BOOKS

NEW YORK LONDON TORONTO SYDNEY SINGAPORE

An *Original* Publication of MTV Books/Pocket Books

POCKET BOOKS, a division of Simon & Schuster, Inc.
1230 Avenue of the Americas, New York, NY 10020

Copyright © 2001 by Meg Castaldo

MTV Music Television and all related titles, logos, and characters are trademarks of MTV Networks, a division of Viacom International Inc.

ISBN: 0-7434-1264-8

First MTV Books/Pocket Books trade paperback printing June 2001

10 9 8 7 6 5 4 3 2 1

POCKET and colophon are registered trademarks of Simon & Schuster, Inc.

Design by Deklah Polansky
Photography by Warren Darius Aftahi

Printed in the U.S.A.

For Andrew,
my partner in crime

_____PART I

chapter 1

Anthony Carmine Orlando had a big round head covered with downy white hair, quick green eyes, and a nose that looked too small for his face. I would've recognized him anywhere. He was planted by the luggage carousel with a cardboard sign that read ALEX ORLANDO in huge block letters. When I said hello, my uncle narrowed his eyes and demanded my middle name. "Rockangela," I replied, slightly embarrassed. He sighed and grabbed my suitcase: "You can't trust anyone in this town."

As it turned out, he was right.

Uncle Carmi hugged me tightly, his stomach taut as a beach ball. Then he cupped my face and said I was beautiful, just like his sister Nin—only without the mustache.

I suppose I ought to explain what I was doing at JFK in the middle of January meeting a relative I hardly knew. The truth was I'd come to break out of a rut. At the ripe age of twenty-eight, I felt stuck. I'd spent six and a half years in college racking up degrees and complicated ideas. In the end, I wound up hustling clothes at Neiman Marcus. From there, I fell into advertising, where I'd been a copy "guru," the poor fool paid to coin persuasive tags for drab T-shirts ("Soft *and* Shiny"—that was mine). I was about to resign when they gave me a pink slip. My boss said: *You're not a team player.* I told him he was wrong: I just didn't like his team.

I blew my severance on a month-long trip to Europe. In Belgium, I got tangled up with Jan, a world-weary gem dealer from Antwerp. I'd always had a thing for foreign men; they weren't from here. By the time I got back to California—broke and restless—I felt like a foreigner myself. I spent a couple of months at my parents' stucco ranch in the flats of Sacramento. I went on interviews. I sent away for law school catalogs—it seemed like a reasonable option. I even dated a dentist they'd proposed. Mostly I was inert. So when the call came from Manhattan—Uncle Carmi was making his annual two-month winter pilgrimage to Puerto Rico (rumor had it he had a "friend" there) and desperately needed a respectable house sitter—I jumped at the chance. Even my parents thought it was a good idea. Who knew such a benign task could become an occupational hazard.

What happened that winter still keeps me up at night. It was the sort of thing no one should ever have to go through. Jan turned out to be a bigger foreigner than I'd ever imagined. My oldest friend, Kyle, became someone I hardly knew. My neighbor Christian unexpectedly left New York. And me? You'd think this mess I'm about to lay out would've opened my eyes. I guess it did. But not in the cathartic way you read about in self-help books. At least I've been cured of my thing for foreign men—well, almost. Now I'm involved with an American. Still, he's a cop, and that's foreign enough for me.

We grabbed my bags from the crowded carousel and climbed into a plush Lincoln Carmi'd hired to take us home. He barked orders at the turbaned driver; I pressed my face against the cool window and tried to catch a glimpse of Queens. On the Long Island Expressway, I saw Manhattan rising in the distance like a sparkling theme park, a promontory of shapely boxes awash with light. It was so beautiful, it took a minute to realize the stars were missing.

Carmi lived in a rent-controlled one bedroom on Twenty-third Street in Chelsea; he'd been there for thirty-five years. As we crossed the threshold to his sixteenth-floor pad, a burst of muffled bickering exploded from the apartment next door. Carmi shook his head and mumbled.

"What was that?" I said.

"The foreigner," he said, as though he'd swallowed something sour.

I heard a woman shout. Carmi frowned. "Some people have no shame."

"Where's she from?" I asked.

"Norway, I think. And she's a *he.*"

He was more interesting than she.

"I want you to be careful while I'm away," Carmi said. "He's a very forward sort of a man."

"Oh, don't worry," I said. I could deal with forward.

Carmi sized me up. I had an altar girl's face—I still got carded—and people tended to trust me on sight.

We stepped onto a black-and-white checkerboard foyer. A dollhouse-size washer-and-drier stood stacked in the corner; fabric softener fragrance hung in the air. Carmi pointed to a three-seater in the next room. "Tonight, you'll sleep here," he said. I thanked him as I took in the overstuffed bookshelves, Atomic Age furniture, a flea market's worth of knickknacks, and thirty-five years of dust.

It seemed like the right time to break out my house-warming gift.

"Well," Carmi said, smiling as he unwrapped the Tanqueray. "Shall we have cocktails? I always have a splash before bed." Today is Tuesday, he explained. Tuesday was gin-and-tonic day. My mother had advised me to bring a bottle of top-shelf gin; clearly she'd been right.

We munched on cheddar and crackers and traded family gossip while cars honked and brakes screeched on the street below. Carmi drained his glass and disappeared into the kitchen to mix another pitcher; round two tasted like napalm. When Carmi suggested a quick tour, I stumbled behind, trying not to embarrass myself.

"Hey, twin beds . . . ," I said, regretting it the moment it slipped out. They were jammed against the bedroom walls and as neatly made as museum pieces. I knew Carmi's roommate of thirteen years had recently passed away.

"I guess they're a bit outmoded," he said.

"Unique," I said. "Not outmoded."

But Carmi wasn't listening. "You don't realize when you're happy . . ." His voice trailed off. Streetlights lit the bedroom, a soft glow filtered through parted curtains.

"Anyway," he said, pulling back the covers on a set of white sheets with blue pinstripes. "I guess I'll turn in." That was my cue. I squeezed his thick forearm. "Thanks for everything."

"Don't mention it," he said, his eyes dusted with memories of his lover.

"Good-night, Uncle Carmi."

"Good-night, Alex," he said. "I'm glad you're here."

"So am I."

By the time I dragged myself out of bed, jet-lagged and hungover, Carmi was gone. It had begun to snow; a light sprinkling of shredded coconut floated in the air. On my suitcase, I found a note: "Stepped out for fresh bagels." The word "fresh" was underlined, twice. I showered, dressed quickly, and brewed coffee. Carmi returned with a heavenly bakery aroma clinging to him like a shadow. I said my perkiest good-morning and handed him a steaming mug.

After breakfast, Carmi sat down at his crowded desk; he had a lot of busy work to complete. He organized papers, wrote checks, made cryptic phone calls, and tidied up. I turned to the crossword puzzle, which was too difficult. Between clues I looked out the window. The sky was an even gray now—it looked cold. I felt like taking a stroll.

I was about to suggest it when Carmi looked accusingly over his shoulder and said: "Louis wasn't at his post this morning, Alex." He shook his head. Louis was one of the doormen. Carmi had dubbed him "Louis the China Man" (because of his slanted Sicilian eyes). "If this should happen while I'm away, I'd like you to phone the management. The number's on my desk." He swiveled in his chair again, hinges squeaking under his weight, and pointed at me. "Always double lock the door and use the chain," he said. "Promise . . ."

I promised. Carmi smiled and returned to his secret work. I thought about all the dumb things I'd done in the past that would've given my uncle a heart attack. I'd hitched rides with strangers, shared sleeping cars with horny Italians, slept in dirty train stations. Nobody knew that stuff about me. Huge eyes and a big toothy grin can do that for you. A Pakistani palmist once told me that my smooth brow foretold a life of dutiful honesty. So far, I'd convinced everyone he was right.

Carmi left in a white linen suit, a straw hat perched on his head, a beat-up leather suitcase in hand. He reminded me of Aschenbach from *Death in Venice*. He hugged me, his cheeks scented like fresh-cut limes. He told me to have fun, which was a surprise. He seemed different, an impostor in my uncle's body. Once he was gone, I bolted the door and lounged on the couch, a novel spread on my chest, the last gasp of sunlight warming my face. I felt like a cat. I dozed off for the next hour. When I finally came to, it was dusk.

Carmi had left a dog-eared guide book scribbled with notes: "Go to D'Ag, don't go Korean market, prices are outrage, go dry cleaner on 8th, worth walk, one cross street Lost My Raincoat!"—and so on. I studied the neighborhood maps. Next to the East Village he'd written: "Don't Go—Very Bad!" in red pen. I read the entry: "St. Marks is an exciting strip of retrograde bohemia." Whatever that meant. Next to the subway map, he'd written in bold letters: "NEVER TAKE SUBWAY. DANGEROUS. USE BUS. See page 13." Since nothing even remotely compromising had ever happened to me, I was pretty certain I'd end up forgetting Carmi's rules. Still, they were fun to read.

My father told me that Carmi had been mugged three times, which helped explain his paranoia. He'd been a cameraman at CBS for most of his adult life, a job that required him to keep ungodly hours. The family considered Carmi harmlessly eccentric. No one knew much about his personal life, other than the fact that he'd had the same roommate for many years and that he loved Puerto Rico. My grandmother always said he was a "good relative," mainly because he sent money on birthdays and for graduations. His gifts were always the first to arrive and the most generous. Before tonight, I'd spent two weeks with him— when I was ten. I didn't remember much about the visit—only that I'd thrown up all over his carpet after scarfing too much calamari in Little Italy.

I checked out Carmi's kitchen. I peered into the tiny fridge, taking in the kosher pickles, six kinds of mustard, sardines packed in oil, and a brown jug of aloe. I rummaged around in the cabinets. They were stacked with cans of garbanzo beans and packets of dehydrated soup. I closed the cupboards. I wouldn't be dipping into Carmi's stash. He was like a Mormon stocking up for the apocalypse. Beside the fridge, I noticed a few paint swatches in varying shades of white tacked to the wall. Was Carmi thinking of redecorating? He didn't strike me as the type.

I headed to the corner Korean market in direct violation of Carmi's edict. Carmi was right: It was expensive. It was also convenient. I ran back to the building, the wind whipping my face like a coarse towel. Maybe it was the new landscape and

Carmi's lingering paranoia, but I had the vague sense that someone was following me. I shifted everything to one hand and pulled the heavy door with the other. Louis was nowhere to be seen. I made a mental note—as per Carmi—to call the management and swiftly forgot. Inside, the heat was blasting. I crossed the dark, brick lobby to the elevators and dropped everything.

As I was unzipping my jacket, I heard a voice behind me.

chapter 2

"You are needing some help?"

I turned around. "Pardon?"

"I saw you coming through." He motioned toward the door with a stack of letters. "I am Christian," he said, extending a little white hand. He was about five nine, fair, well fed, and definitely not American.

The elevator doors opened. He swept up my bags and we stepped inside. "You are living in my floor," he said. It was more a statement than a question. "I heard you this morning, very early." He smiled at me. I nodded, thinking he was pleasant-looking enough, though I didn't like the idea of someone eavesdropping. Then it hit me: He was Carmi's foreigner.

"You are living with Mr. Carmi?" he asked.

"He's my uncle," I said. "I'm staying here while he's away."

"Ah, yes," he said. "In the Puerto Rico."

How he knew this was beyond me. Carmi didn't strike me as the type to broadcast plans. We rode in silence; the elevator crept along. I tried to place his accent.

"Have you been?" he asked.

"Sorry?" I said.

"Puerto Rico?"

"No," I said, wondering what he was getting at. "Have you?"

"Nooo," he squealed. "Puerto Rico is very far from Sweden."

His high-pitched giggle was oddly girlish. "Yes," I said. "It is."

"You are not looking like a Puerto Rican," he said.

I laughed. It was the first of many idiotic things I'd hear from Christian. "And what does a Puerto Rican look like?"

"I do not know," he said, unflappable. He appraised me thoughtfully. "But not like you. You are looking like a Greek or Egyptian."

"Imaginative," I said. I'd been mistaken for every olive race on the planet. But I wasn't going to tell him.

"You are of the Jewish faith?" he asked, shifting his weight from one penny loafer to the other.

I laughed, again. "No," I said. "I'm afraid not." It reminded me of an episode in London. My cousin and I were waiting to get into a crowded bar. Three guys pulled up in a yellow Porsche and silently grabbed us by the arms. Before we could protest they dragged us to a table, handed us drinks, and bombarded us with Hebrew. When we opened our mouths and our booming American voices came out, they were shocked, though not, I suppose, disappointed. It's amazing the confusion a complexion can cause.

The elevator doors parted. He picked up my bags and followed me to Carmi's. I unlocked the door, nudging it open with my shoe. "I can handle these," I said. "Thanks."

"I am a friend of your uncle," he said, grinning.

Carmi hadn't implied they were friends. All I knew was that Carmi said he was forward, which he was. For the first time, I took a good look at this Christian. He was young and sort of handsome, his nose a perfect turned-up number, his cheeks smooth and round like two scoops of vanilla ice cream. He had a mop of blond frizzy curls. "I'll tell him you said hello," I lied. I had an urge to call him Tadzio.

"Welcome to this building," he said.

"Thanks."

I was about to close the door when I noticed Christian's mouth ajar. I hesitated. He took advantage and cut in: "Maybe you would like to take something to drink?" He took a few steps back. "On another day, of course?"

"Maybe," I said. It was my usual noncommittal response. I knew it was probably better to say no, but I didn't have the heart.

Besides, he was sort of charming. Christian's face lit up like a fire had ignited in his mind. I smiled without showing any teeth. "Well, good-bye," I said, firmly shutting the door. As I unpacked my groceries, I tried to guess how soon he'd be back.

Around eleven, the phone startled me. I waited for the answering machine to pick up; then I changed my mind. I thought it might be Carmi, checking up on me from Puerto Rico—to make sure I hadn't gone to the Korean market. The moment I heard Kyle's voice, I knew my life was about to get a lot more complicated.

"Hey," he said. It was his standard greeting.

"Hey, yourself." I wanted to ask how he'd gotten this number. But I didn't bother. He'd have some crazy story.

"Come down to Twelfth and B."

"Where's that?"

"East Village."

"Oh."

Going would mean breaking another one of Carmi's rules. My uncle would be disappointed.

"Come down to Twelfth and B," he repeated.

"Why?"

"So you can meet her." He dropped the phone.

"Who?" I waited, the line crackling. I heard Spanish. "Who?"

"What?"

"I can barely hear you," I said irritably.

"Why not?"

"I don't know."

"Are you coming down?"

"No."

He was silent, then: "Later." He slammed the receiver in my ear.

"Bastard," I said to the dead line. I slammed down the receiver, too, but with little satisfaction.

I'd known Kyle Hangerman for eleven years. We'd gone to high school together in Sacramento. Back then, he was gangly with a coat of freckles, bad skin, and spiked auburn hair that jutted from his square head like porcupine quills. At sixteen, he'd read everything and was interested in nothing. He was smart but he was lost. By the time we met, he was already sniffing glue in the pasture behind his house. Back then, I thought he was different. When I think about it now, I guess I found him fascinating, like an exotic creature you'd dig up in a rain forest.

What Kyle saw in me wasn't exactly clear. I was a loner. And like him I wasn't very popular. Kyle could've cared less. So we found each other, as outsiders sometimes do, and we stuck together, despising everyone for despising us. We never had sex, not even a kiss. He didn't have the nerve, and I couldn't imagine it. It would've been like screwing your brother.

When I was shipped off to college, Kyle skipped town to wander the country. He became a regular vagabond, always unhappy, always searching for a profound experience, something or someone to show him the way. He'd call me, collect, usually in the middle of the night from a place I'd never been—Baton Rouge, Detroit, Buffalo. Sometimes every night for a week; sometimes once a month. He was full of tales: He'd been a snake charmer, a sword-swallowing apprentice, a gigolo, a carny, a zookeeper, a dope dealer, a dope addict, and so on. Over the years, I saw him less and less. And when I did, we were both surprised by the fact that he'd become a man and I was a woman. But it didn't matter. Sometimes I'd think he was the one person in the world who actually knew me.

chapter 3

The doorbell rang the next morning around ten. I wondered who could be calling on me so early. Stupidly, I opened the door without latching the chain. Christian introduced himself as though we'd never met and strolled elegantly into the foyer like he'd been here before. I let him stay, if only out of curiosity.

Christian looked as if he'd been out all night. He had on a wrinkled suit; his beard was russet and stubbly. Still, he was sort of sexy—a kind of careless boyishness, like no one had told him to wash up. He stretched his legs in Carmi's kitchen while I waited for the coffee to perk.

"You are liking New York?" he asked.

"So far," I said. "I just got here." I hadn't really been anywhere. But I wasn't going to tell him.

"Yah," he said. "I like New York. The atmosphere."

I poured the coffee; it was pitch-black.

"Where are you from?" he asked.

"California," I said. "Where are you from?"

"I told you, Sweden."

"I forgot," I said, sitting across from him. I knew he was Scandinavian—but Carmi had said he was Norwegian.

"You are involved?" He held my eyes for a moment, his milk-white skin turned red as grenadine.

It took me a minute to catch on. "With someone?"

He nodded. Carmi was right: He was forward.

"I was wondering," he said, stumbling a little.

"I was wondering that myself."

"Only you can know," he said, excitedly.

"You're right," I said. "Only I can know."

He didn't say anything more. He was trying to make out what I was telling him. "Do not take me the wrong way," he said, dragging his words together. "I do not mean. You do not have to say. I am only making talk. My English is sometimes . . ." He cleared his throat. "Is not so good." He smiled at me with the lightest brown eyes I'd ever seen, eyes that gave you nothing at all, not one shred of emotion. "Forgive me," he said. "I am apologizing."

He was overdoing it, but I liked his gift for self-deprecating; it was a good quality. "It's okay." I was hardly offended.

"But," he said. There was always a but. "It's just that you are acting nervous. I am watching you and you are moving your leg a lot."

I stopped. He'd almost embarrassed me. "I'm not nervous," I said, though I hadn't noticed my leg moving. "I have a lot of . . . energy."

"'Energy,'" he repeated, whispering the word like he didn't know what it meant. Maybe there wasn't a Swedish translation. Christian leaned back in his seat and draped an arm on the windowsill; he pretended to study the street. I glanced at my watch. I thought about Carmi. What did he have on this Scandinavian dandy?

"How do you know my uncle?"

"I am only knowing him a little," he said, still gazing out the window.

"But you know him."

He smiled at me. "I will explain you another time."

What was there to explain? "Tell me."

He finished his coffee in one long gulp. "It is nothing really. We had some drinks together. That is all."

I couldn't quite picture them tossing back martinis, but weirder things had happened. Christian crossed the tiny kitchen to the sink and filled his cup with tap water. He had a tiny O-shaped mouth and pretty, iridescent skin, the kind of complexion men compliment women for. He shoved his hands in his pockets.

"I guess I am going."

"Okay," I said. He'd stayed for only twenty minutes.

"I have to meet a client."

"What do you do anyway?"

"I am an architect. I studied at the Columbia." He pointed out the window as though the Columbia was across the street. "I am designing things for many New Yorkers."

"That's why you came here?"

He nodded, a puff of curls falling across his forehead.

On his way out, he brushed passed me, letting his hand graze my thigh ever so slightly. So perfect was his discretion I thought I had imagined his touch.

chapter 4

I got a job at Barneys. It was the first position I'd applied for. They were thrilled I'd learned the ropes at Neiman Marcus and hired me on the spot. The next morning, I found myself marooned in a department called the CO/OP, a boxy sunken living room that was generally considered the lamest section of the store. Here, the prices were comparatively low; you had to sell a truckload just to make decent commission. My new boss, Olga, had worked at Barneys for eight years, a fact she revealed to me without the slightest trace of regret.

"You can straighten these racks," Olga said, her stout body stuffed into a slick rubber getup. Her orange crew cut was as rough as a floor brush. I didn't particularly enjoy my new task, but it seemed unwise to get on her bad side. I straightened. Olga watched to make sure I got the hang of it.

After about an hour, customers started rolling in. Olga let out a snort, her bull nostrils flaring. Then she began to sell—everything and anything. I could've cared less, except that I'd have to do the same if I wanted to make any money. Minus the commission, my salary was paltry. I sized up every wide-eyed pilgrim, trying to clock who was loaded and who was looking. By lunch, Olga had only out-sold me by three hundred bucks.

"You've done this before," she said, riffling through a stack of receipts.

"Yeah," I said. "In another life."

She shook a receipt in front of my face. "I want to tell you something." She appraised me with her mean black eyes. "You sold to *my* client."

"What?"

"You sold to Helene Finckle." She waved the receipt as though I'd remember who she was.

"Sorry," I said. That was life in the fast lane.

"She's my client," Olga said, her voice rising. "For future reference."

"I didn't know," I said. "What would you like me to do about it?"

"She likes me to help her."

"She didn't ask for you."

"That doesn't matter."

Olga was right about that. It didn't matter. Nothing in this place mattered. When I took the gig I figured no one in their right mind would try to make a mission of it—unlike the agency I used to work for, where a tag line for an ad was a matter of life and death. But Olga was proving me wrong.

"She's my client." Olga touched her chest with a long orange nail. "Got that?"

"I'll try to remember."

"Yeah," she said. "Maybe you ought to make a list."

"Oh," I said, trying to follow her twisted mind. "As a reference?"

She brightened up at this. "Yeah . . . so you don't get confused."

"Alright," I said, taking a note card out of a drawer. At the top, I wrote in big retard letters: OLGA'S CLIENTS. #1 HELENE FINCKLE. Then I folded it into a square, slipped it in my pocket, and smiled. Olga seemed pleased. Then she sent me downstairs—for sock-and-hat duty. I was glad to get away from her. Still, I wondered who else was in store for me. It didn't take long to find out.

As I was opening the second register (a task, per Olga, that had to be done for the afternoon shift), a short pudgy guy in a loden-green plaid suit and navy bow tie stalked into the department. He gave me the once-over.

"Malcolm Foxman," he said. "Welcome to drudgery."

"Thanks," I said. "Alex Orlando."

"Oh," he said. "Italian." His eyes were obscured by huge tortoise-shell frames. "I had you pegged as something more exotic. Persian, maybe."

"Sorry to let you down," I said, taking in his cutting tone.

"It's not your fault. Everything is so banal anyway."

What a barrel of laughs he was going to be.

"What are you doing?" he asked, peering over those ridiculous glasses.

"Opening."

"Well, you're not doing it right."

"Says who?" I could certainly follow directions.

"You're doing it the long way," he said, sidling next to me.

"Be my guest." I didn't know there was a short way.

Malcolm studied the receipt hanging from the register. He shook his head, plucked a few keys with a stubby index finger, and slapped the money in the till. I inched away; his clothes reeked of cigarettes. In two minutes it was done. He slammed the register drawer shut. "There," he said.

"Thanks for the lesson."

He cracked a smile, a pleasant flash across his sullen face. Then he beetled over to the socks-and-tights tables. I noticed he walked with a slight limp, dragging a pair of shiny black boots with thick heels. Orthopedic maybe. Every so often he would stop before a cube of knee-highs, yank them out, and furiously refold them. I'd hoped Malcolm would be more fun than Olga. But I guess you couldn't ask for much given the circumstances.

"Are you going to hold up that counter all day or what?"

I picked up the credit card applications and stacked them; I tossed a few stray pens into a drawer. "I'm tidying," I said.

Another smile, more of a frown really. "You can go to the

stockroom and get ten pounds of these," he said, flinging a pair of black wool tights in my direction. "We don't have any large. And believe me, when those beasts from the Island start pouring in we'll need plenty." He scrunched up his nose like something stunk and began stalking the jewelry cases. "And don't dawdle," he said, shaking a finger at me. "It's nearly time for my afternoon constitutional." He took a pack of Pall Malls out of his pocket.

I grabbed the tights and stomped off to the stockroom. I was beginning to think I should've gotten a job at Macy's. All I wanted was to secure a little coin so I wouldn't have to go back to California penniless and face the horror of moving back into my kiddy room with the lavender-flowered wallpaper. I hoped I'd make it—two months was a long time.

"I said to *hurry.*" Malcolm's shrill voice sent needles into my skin. "I'm going into hysterics." His features morphed into a series of constipated grimaces; maybe he was an actor. His dramatic gifts were pretty convincing.

"Calm down," I said. "I couldn't find them."

Before I could say anything more, Malcolm was on his way out, his heavy boots dragging underfoot. I saw him outside, pacing in front of the window, black wavy hair bobbing up and down between the mannequins, ribbons of gray smoke drifting above his head.

I'd soon learn that Malcolm Foxman was in fact a minor playwright of some renown; a newspaper review of one of his plays was tacked above the register. In the photo, Malcolm wore a plaid suit that looked more like a Catholic school uniform. His mouth was drawn into a straight line, his hands rested on his lap. He seemed like he was waiting to confess. The review said Malcolm had a caustic sense of humor; the recurring theme in his absurdist plays was a castrating mother figure. It also said

Malcolm was razor-sharp, his mind an agile Slinky. In the few minutes we'd worked together, this came as no surprise.

We spent the rest of the day selling worthless things: hats that would fly off on windy days; bathing gear cum space suits, overpriced jewelry, fancy facial creams that promised to turn back the clock. Malcolm watched my every move. By six thirty or so the place was empty again. He went back to his compulsive straightening. I found myself alongside, more for company than anything else.

"I hate it when someone else sells more than me," he said.

"You don't have to worry," I said. "I won't."

"That's what they all say at first."

"I'm saying it and I mean it."

"That's just dandy," he said, clomping to the handbag piazza. I watched him tear apart the display. Maybe when he realized I wasn't going to steal his clients or his one-liners, he'd warm up a little and we could at least be civil. Olga swung by to check our sales. Malcolm had four thousand in; I'd done about three. Pleased with himself, he offered his third smile of the day. Would I please close out both registers? He was late for a meeting with his producer.

chapter 5

When I got back from work, I saw Christian in the lobby talking quietly to a woman. She had almond skin and a fringe of shiny black hair. When she smiled at him, her teeth were the color of egg shells. She was standing close to Christian—so close I figured they were more than friends. I pretended not to notice and turned to Carmi's mailbox. There wasn't much for him—a bunch of credit card offers. And . . . a letter from Jan, for me. When I saw his handwriting, I felt a nervous twitter. I hadn't heard from him in a while; I'd begun to wonder if he'd forgotten our fling. I'd sent him my New York address so that he'd write to me, if only to fend off loneliness. My mother planned to write once a week. I liked receiving letters. There was something reassuring about seeing your name on an envelope.

When I reached the elevator, Christian was holding the door for me, his finger glued to the Door Open button. He was alone. I could practically hear the wheels spinning in his fair head. Christian was trying to decide if he ought to mention the woman. Another thirty seconds passed.

"Thank you again for the coffee," he said.

"It's nothing."

He hesitated, glancing at me furtively.

"Your finger must be tired," I said.

Christian let the button go. "Yes," he said, laughing. "I was forgetting where I am going."

We watched the numbers light up: 2, 3, 4, 5, 6.

"Tomorrow you will take some dinner with me?" he asked, his voice rising with every word.

"I can't," I said. "I'm busy." I didn't want him to think I had nothing to do, even if I didn't.

"Of course you can," he insisted, as if everything had been settled. "I will come for you about eight thirty, okay?"

"I can't," I said again.

He frowned. He was not to be turned down. "But you can."

Looking back now, this was my big chance to blow Christian off; to keep him out of my life for good. The problem was I sort of liked him. It was hard to admit, but there was something about him that intrigued me. It wasn't like I had a ton of other offers. That was reason enough to give in. I said I'd think about it. Predictably, he took that as a yes.

"Then it is settled," Christian said triumphantly, as the elevator opened. He turned and headed toward his apartment. "See you tomorrow," he said. He closed the door and was gone.

I fished Jan's letter out of my jacket and tore it open. It was short, a couple of paragraphs jotted on flimsy blue airmail paper. The letter said Jan was coming to New York in about ten days. He had some business here; he wanted to see me again. If I didn't want to see him, he'd understand. He gave me the date and a flight number. I could meet him at the airport, if I'd like. He'd be staying at a hotel. That's all he said. His restraint appealed to my nineteenth-century taste; I was left to imagine the rest. I tried to find something between the lines. But I couldn't. Jan didn't gush feelings like a broken pipe. That's what I'd liked about him in the first place.

I took a shower and examined myself in the fogged mirror, wondering if I'd look any different to Jan. It had been more than six months since I'd seen him. My hair was longer; my skin drained of its California tan. Sitting down, you'd think I was tall. But I wasn't. I was small-boned with a swanlike neck. I had a slightly scrawny figure, and from certain angles, I could pass for a ballerina or an adolescent boy. I had dark eyes, good cheek-bones, and big teeth. Nothing in itself was remarkable. No one ever said I had nice eyes or great hair or lovely skin. Everything just lined up properly.

Once, at Neiman Marcus, a female colleague had asked me: "How does it feel to be beautiful?" When people think you're beautiful, you work at being nice. You're always perceived as the competition, as the woman with the most exciting life, all because your features fell in the right places. The woman who'd asked the question was pretty herself, her face not unlike a Botticelli angel. I laughed it off. I wasn't really so exceptional-looking at all, I said. Mostly, being beautiful was overrated.

I took out two photos of Jan: a flattering profile I'd taken in front of the Basilica of the Holy Blood; another at an inn in Ghent that caught two-thirds of his face. It reminded me of his peculiar allure. He had the sort of looks that were arresting in their oddity. Even if Jan was peering straight into the lens, he wouldn't have given much away. If anything, that was what made me want to see him again.

I could picture him now. I could picture myself. We were back at the Bahnhof Zoo in Berlin. It was late last summer. We'd met because I couldn't speak German. He saw me struggling with the agent. I kept saying: *Ich spreche kein Deutsch.* Jan stepped in and arranged my train ticket. He was more striking than hand-some, his face as angular as a cubist painting. It was his eyes though—pale blue, almost colorless—that hooked me. And I was drawn enough to drink and talk a day away in a cafe some-where in Kurfürstendamm, our knees brushing under the table. It turned out that Jan was a gem dealer and his work took him all over the world; he'd been to places I'd longed to visit but might never see—Goa, Johannesburg. By dusk, I felt like I'd known him a long time. Outside the cafe, he gave me his card. If

I came to Belgium, I should call him. When he touched my arm to say good-bye, his hand was on fire.

We spent four days in Brugge in an inn with blue shutters on the windows and bicycles parked out front. We drank a lot and strolled around the Markt. And we made love. It was different somehow: slow and methodical, not exactly passionless, but languid like the country itself. It was also monastically quiet—something I'd never experienced before or since. Saying good-bye was harder than I expected. I thought I could fall in love with him. But that was a long time ago.

Before I hit the sack, I found a sheet of stationery and scribbled a page of love-sick blather to Jan. I tore that up and started again. I tried about three times before I wrote something that didn't sound ridiculous. I didn't say more than he had said—just that I wanted to see him again, too. I sealed the envelope, pasted a few first-class stamps above his name, and marched it down to the mailbox. I wasn't sure if my letter would reach him in time. As soon as the lid slammed shut, I felt sick. Maybe I'd been too hasty.

When I got back upstairs, there was a message from Carmi saying that he'd arrived safely. I could barely hear his voice over the static in the background. He said something about picking up a package—or so it sounded. His voice was so garbled I couldn't make out what he was asking; the machine cut him off. I deleted his message. I was sure he'd be calling again soon enough. He could tell me then.

chapter 6

The next evening, Christian and I were in a crowded French cafe ripe with the odor of roasted meat, stale cigarettes, and spilled wine. We had a cramped corner table. Christian lounged on his banquette in a pressed black suit, scanning the room as though he expected someone. I could barely hear him over the clatter of cutlery and drunken laughter. I'd almost given up on conversation.

"You know," he said, excitedly, leaning across the table. "I see a lot of the movie star and model here."

"Really?" I said. I wasn't all that interested but I didn't want to hurt his feelings.

"Yah," he said. "This is a very stylish place."

I craned my neck so I could take in the room. "I don't see anyone famous."

"Not tonight," he said. "But it is cool when I see the American movie star and the model." He took a sip of water. "I tell my friends in Sweden and they are very impressed."

"Well," I said, opening my menu. "I guess you don't see too many stars in Stockholm."

"No," he said. "Just the Abba."

A waiter finally made it to our table. Christian asked me if he could order for us. I said I didn't mind. He showed off his French. My French was so abysmal I wasn't sure if he was actually doing it right. The waiter seemed annoyed; he kept bending over and saying, *"What?"*

When he left, Christian said, "You are liking life in New York?"

Since he'd already asked me this question and obviously forgotten, I gave him my standard answer. "So far." I didn't tell him I hadn't done much except get a job, stick my head into a few galleries, and pick up groceries. "Do *you* like it?" I asked.

"I like New York very much," he said. "You know, I go to club, to restaurant, to theater. It is all very nice . . ." Christian took a slug of wine, his face was flushed like he'd just run ten miles. "You are thinking?"

"I'm always thinking," I said. I had Jan on my mind. He'd be here soon.

"What about?"

"All kinds of stuff."

"What stuff are you referring?"

"I got some news today."

Christian seemed alarmed. "From Mr. Carmi?"

I shook my head. I could picture Jan reading my letter while I was flirting with a stranger. "No," I said. "Not from Carmi."

A waiter plopped a foie gras terrine in front of us. Christian delved into it, smacking his greasy lips. I took a bite. It melted on my tongue like caramel.

"What is the news then?" Christian said, blotting his forehead with a handkerchief.

I gave him a few sketchy details about Jan. Christian seemed relieved. "It is okay," he said. "My *friend* is visiting, too."

"The woman in the lobby?" I said, her pretty face coming back to me.

Christian refilled his glass, his eyes sparkly for a change. "What woman are you referring?" He smiled slyly. I could tell he liked being caught.

"Oh, come on," I said, playing along. "The one I saw."

The harried waiter dropped off another round. Christian tore into his faux filet with gusto. "She used to be my girlfriend," he said, between mouthfuls.

It figured. That explained the bickering.

"It does not matter now," he continued, his lips shinning as if they were glossed.

the foreigner_____**MEG CASTALDO**

"And why is that?"

"I am not loving her," he sighed, leaning back in his chair, utensils pointing toward the ceiling. "She wanted to get married. But her parents are strict. She is from Algeria. They have a man already picked out for her."

"An arranged marriage," I said, marveling at the idea.

He nodded. "It is okay," he said, patting my hand. "She is too easy for me. She is always trying to please." He giggled. "I can be very bad you know." He attacked his faux filet again as though he'd just been absolved. I tried to eat my steak, but it was like shoe leather. I was thinking about that woman and her arranged marriage. It was exotic in the most medieval of ways.

"When is she going back to Algeria?" I said.

"Who?"

"Your ex-girlfriend—what other Algerians do you know?"

Christian gave his tie a yank and unbuttoned his collar. "You are asking a lot of questions," he said. "Eat your dinner now."

"I'm full," I said, pushing my plate away and holding his gaze for an answer.

"I am not sure," he said. "Whenever she wants." He shook his head. "Americans," he said. "They are always wanting the answers."

I was just trying to make conversation. "Then you ask the questions," I said.

He brightened up at this. "When is Mr. Carmi coming from the Puerto Rico?"

"Not for two months," I said, wondering why he was so interested in Carmi. "He doesn't like the cold."

"Yes," he said, grinning. "I know."

"How do you know?"

"Now you are asking the questions, again," he said, pushing back his empty plate.

"I'm sorry."

"I already told you," he said. "I am only knowing Mr. Carmi a little."

The dessert tray rolled by; I ordered a chocolate mousse.

We dug in, our spoons banging together. Christian began talking about his work. Something about the way he described his projects made me wonder if he was lying. I couldn't put my finger on it.

When we got back to the apartment, Christian wanted to come in. I wasn't surprised—he probably felt a kiss was payback for dinner. I said I wasn't feeling too well, which was actually true. The wine had gone to my head. Christian didn't plead. In fact, he conducted himself like a perfect little gentleman. Only his gleaming eyes and inflamed skin gave him away. Then he smiled, thanked me for joining him, and kissed me on both cheeks. Before I could say anything more, he was gone.

chapter 7

I was swapping my work clothes for jeans and a T-shirt when the buzzer rang. Through the peephole, I saw Kyle leaning against the wall, one knee poking forward, a regular mutant James Dean. I knew it was just a matter of time. He'd popped up like he always did, without bothering to call. It was typical Kyle. All the same, it was good to see a familiar face. Or almost familiar. Hard living had begun to catch up with him. There were faint creases around his hazel eyes; his auburn hair was twisted in thick shoulder-length knots. His beat-up clothes hung on his rangy six-foot frame. He seemed even taller; maybe because he was skinnier than I'd ever seen him. I tried not to look too concerned. But he must've noticed.

"What are you gawking at?" he said.

"I don't think I've seen you for a year," I said. "You've changed."

"I'm gettin' uglier all the time," he said, hugging me as if I was about to disappear. He smelled of soap and tobacco—like he always did.

"What are you looking at?" I said.

"You."

"What about me?"

"You're still pretty."

"Like you expected me to be ugly?"

"No," he said, a laugh escaping. "But I wish you would be."

"Sorry." We were still in the foyer, readjusting to one another.

"Then you'd have to marry me."

I groaned. "Never."

"Why not?" he demanded.

"Because I couldn't."

"We'd have a smart kid."

"Maybe," I said, picturing myself lying on a gurney covered with sweat, Kyle's child kicking and screaming to stay inside me. When he was born, Kyle weighed more than thirteen pounds; he'd nearly killed his mother. It was something he was proud of.

"This your uncle's crib?" he said, stepping into the living room.

"Yeah."

"You should see where I live." He started laughing, deep and raspy.

"I can imagine."

"No, you can't," he said, rolling his eyes as if I'd said something dumb. He wandered around, poking his head in the kitchen. "Yassi's place is a dump."

Kyle had been calling me pretty consistently before I'd come east. I'd heard all about Yassi; she was the latest in a series of borderline mental cases. He'd always told me about his exotic girlfriends, whether I was interested or not. After I returned from Europe, I'd filled Kyle in on Jan but I doubted he remembered. Kyle was always jealous of my amorous pursuits. For him, finding happiness was a competition. And he played to win. The thought of me being happier than him—for whatever reason— tended to make Kyle crazy with envy.

"How's Yassi?" I said.

"That bitch," he mumbled. "I'm gonna kill her."

Kyle had said she was going back to France. "I thought she was leaving?"

"She'll never leave me," he said, shaking his head. "I won't let her."

I almost felt sorry for her. Trapped by Kyle.

"What about you?" he said. "Meet anyone yet?"

I wouldn't tell Kyle about Jan's letter. "Just my neighbor," I said. "Christian."

"What's up with him?"

"Another Euro," I said. "You know me."

Kyle nodded. "If he starts buggin' you," he said, "I'll kick his ass."

Typical Kyle bravado. "Don't bother," I said. "I don't need you in jail on my account."

We ended up in Carmi's room. Kyle flopped on a bed and the mattress shuddered. He stared at the ceiling, his legs splayed. "Sit here," he said, patting a tiny half-moon near him. As usual, Kyle wanted to be close to me, maybe to prove that I was really alive. I understood the impulse. It was disconcerting to reattach a warm body to what had become a memory. I sat on the bed. He slid his long fingers under my hair, stroking the fuzz on the nape of my neck. "You're so skinny," he said, squeezing. "I'd forgotten." He squeezed harder. I imagined my skin turning white.

"Hey," I said, batting his hand away.

"I could break your neck in one snap."

"That's comforting."

He gave me a playful push. "Don't be so serious." Hanging around Kyle was like putting up with a kid brother.

Kyle wanted to go to the Gold Room, where Yassi supposedly worked the bar, which meant, of course, free booze. He pleaded with me until I gave in, nostalgia winning me over again.

At the Gold Room, Yassi was nowhere in sight. Kyle didn't bother to explain; I didn't ask. We hovered near the dilapidated bar and ordered beer. Iggy Pop pounded in my ears: *I wanna be your dog.* The place was cramped. Couches lined the decrepit walls. The light was dim; clouds of smoke clung to the ceiling. Kyle lit a cigarette and looked around—for Yassi I figured—though he didn't say. Every so often he would reach over and hug me. I felt like a teenager again, which was unsettling. I seemed to be quickly regressing in every area of my life: the Barneys gig, Kyle, even Jan. I tried not to think about it.

"I thought Yassi was going to be here," I said.

"What?"

"I said I thought Yassi was going to be here."

He shrugged. "Maybe she quit."

Kyle ordered a shot and two more beers. He hadn't changed a bit. It could've been depressing if it wasn't also comforting. Kyle turned to lean over a scrawny, shabby-looking guy. I couldn't make out what they were saying—the Ramones this time. Then Kyle slid off his stool and stretched his arms above his head, a glint in his eye.

"This is Rob," he said, smacking the red-faced guy on the stomach.

Rob grinned, showing two rows of corn teeth. "What's up?" he said.

I smiled slightly.

"He's got some stuff," Kyle said. "You want to come?"

I didn't ask what stuff because I already knew. "No," I said. "You go."

He paused for a minute, a quick tug-of-war running through his head: me or a thrill. It wasn't a tough choice for Kyle. "I'll call you," he said.

"See you," I said. Corn Teeth nodded my way. I pretended not to notice. I didn't need any more friends. They pushed their way through the crowd. I swiveled back around to the bar, intent on finishing the third beer that I hadn't wanted in the first place. I took two more sips and left.

The street was deserted. My ears were ringing. It was past one thirty. How had it gotten so late? I was somewhere in the East Village. Carmi'd be disappointed when they found my body here. I could've been in Beirut for all I knew—even the litter looked odd. I didn't have enough money for a cab. That idiot Kyle had drank it all. There weren't any around anyway. I hustled to the corner, kicking myself for not paying attention to where he'd taken me. I cursed Kyle, stomping my feet to keep the cold from numbing my toes. I looked around again and decided I ought to move. Standing around like a fool didn't help.

I swung around a corner a lot faster than usual. Two guys were hanging out on a graffiti-covered stoop. I couldn't see their faces. One of them said something to me. I could've sworn I heard my name, but I wrote it off as a hallucination, like the feeling of being followed. I was almost running now, the voice behind me nipped my heels. I felt a hand on my shoulder. I whirled around, breathing like a sprinter, ready to be mugged or raped or killed. Kyle's wind-burned face towered over me.

"Where the fuck are you going?" he said.

"Home," I said, mopping up my relieved forehead.

"Why you headed this way?"

"I like the scenic route."

He couldn't help but laugh. Bastard that he was.

"I'll walk you back in a minute," he said, glancing up the block. "I'm just waitin' on my man Rob."

The beer had clobbered me. I was freezing. I wanted to get back to Carmi's. I turned on my heel again. Kyle grabbed my arm.

"You're not going the right way." A grin spread across his freckle-splattered face. "Just wait a sec. I'll be right back." He rushed to the corner, hands shoved in his pockets. I stood on a stained patch of sidewalk near a pock-marked bodega. I couldn't move, even if wanted to. I was turning to marble, my fingers stiff inside my gloves. Kyle hurried back, fiddling with the zipper on his jacket.

"Let's get outta here," he said, looking around as if he half-expected to get busted. He practically ran down the street. I paid attention this time. It didn't take me long to figure out that we weren't heading back to Carmi's. Next thing I knew, I was following Kyle up the steps of a crumbling walk-up.

"This is it," Kyle said. "Thanks for walking *me* home." He let out a gaggle of laughter.

I was too pissed to think of a good comeback. And I was too tired to wander around anymore. I went in, calling him an asshole, which only broke him up more. We hiked up five flights; Kyle moving two stairs at a time with his long, skinny legs. The gray tile floor was gritty under my boots; the rickety banisters tacky under my hands. Faded Christmas decorations were taped to some of the doors: a paper wreath, Santa Claus, a reindeer. Kyle was waiting in front of an open door. "Hurry up," he said, looking down at me. I moved even slower. "Fuck you," I said.

The apartment stunk. "It smells like someone died," I said. "Open a window."

We were in a dimly lit kitchen; a leaky faucet echoed in the tiny space. On my right, there was a pile of books, a lamp without a shade, and two naked pillows on the floor. "Come this way," Kyle said, dragging me into another room with an unmade bed, a purple velvet chair, and a second lamp with a pink fringe shade. He was right: It was a dump.

Kyle squatted on the mattress and untied a neat brown package, his knicked fingers working furiously.

He paused for a moment to look up at me. "Sit down."

"I want to go." I still hadn't taken off my coat.

"Wait," he said, sprinkling a taste on the back of his hand. He snorted it, throwing his head back. I flopped on the chair and unzipped my coat. We weren't going anywhere now. I watched

the foreigner_____MEG CASTALDO

Kyle suck up all the powder. I'd given up sermonizing long ago. It wasn't any use. He'd only laugh and tell me to lighten up.

"It's pretty lame," he said, wiping a string of snot from his nose.

"I don't really care."

"You get the best stuff uptown."

"I'll keep that in mind," I said.

Kyle stretched out on the bed. Soon he was breathing like a toddler, his cheeks flushed. He was lost in himself, comatose. I couldn't believe the idiotic course of events that had led me here. I had a vision of Yassi coming home to find me parked on her prissy chair. I didn't want to meet anyone like this, with Kyle in a stupor on the bed. But I was pretty sure I couldn't find my way back to Carmi's.

I tried to get comfortable, but a metal coil pressed into my ass. Kyle's revenge. I pulled my legs underneath me. I didn't even bother to take off my boots. I picked up a battered book by Conrad and flipped through it. Kyle had underlined:

Only in men's imagination does every truth find an effective and undeniable existence. Imagination not invention, is the supreme master of art as of life.

As far as I was concerned, fate was a close second. Why else would I be trapped in Yassi's bedroom? Kyle had scrawled notes in the margin, but his handwriting was illegible. I fought to keep my eyes open, but the beer was sloshing through my veins like a lullaby. Eventually, I nodded off, the sound of Kyle's heavy breathing in my ears.

chapter 8

Malcolm was late. For the past three hours, he'd been calling to say he was on his way. I'd told him not to worry—I could hold down the fort. Business was slow; we'd just be fighting over crumbs. But Malcolm was chemically incapable of not worrying. And of not showing up.

He finally arrived in a wrinkled plaid suit with a crooked yellow bow tie, his pale face peppered with wiry black stubble. "I was up all night," he declared, perking up his Spockian ears. "I'm a writing fool." He looked like he'd been up for days: he had bed-head and his eyes were bloodshot. He opened his briefcase. "Here," he said, tossing a manuscript into my arms. "For your reading pleasure. You should know what kind of people you're selling girdles with."

I marveled at his professionalism. The play was single spaced and typed in a tiny font. I told Malcolm he obviously had a lot to say. He said if my childhood was as horrific as his, I could go on about it for decades, too. Once, I'd dabbled at writing myself. Mostly I started things and let them rot. A few years ago, I'd published a short story called the "Great White Ape"— loosely about Kyle—in a literary journal. That was the high point of my career. "I'm impressed," I said. As usual he took it the wrong way. "I'm a playwright," he spat out. "What do you think this is?" Then he furiously refolded a unitard. It was hard to imagine Ibsen doing such things.

"It might be interesting to get *your* opinion," he said. "I don't know many people who can actually read."

There was a reason for everything. "I'm honored."

Malcolm stopped folding and scrunched up his face. "Don't say such silly things." He tore apart the sock display. "And when you're praising it, remember to cite my looks. Not everyone can be brilliant *and* beautiful."

"Yes," I said. "You know how text-driven I am."

"You can take it home and read it like a bedtime story."

"I can't wait." I scanned the title page—KITTY KATS AND KLEPTOMANIACS, BY MALCOLM R. FOXMAN. Maybe I was selling socks with a genius. In a hundred years, he'd be the garmento G. B. Shaw.

"It's brilliant—if I do say so myself."

Nothing like modesty. Still, I was flattered that he wanted me to read it. He thought more of me than he'd let on. Malcolm wasn't big on showing anything vaguely like real emotion. That'd be too dangerous.

"You have two days," he said.

"For what?"

"To read it, of course."

I didn't think manuscripts had expiration dates. "I'll get right on it."

During lunch I found out that the characters had names like Star Spangled, Tofu Jackson, and Peter Piper. Act I was called: "Variations on Forgetting Who You Are and How You Came to Be What You Forgot." The play was obviously based on his life. Malcolm blamed his parents for everything, from his mother's bad taste to the shaky-handed mohel his father had picked "to butcher me." He later told me that he'd been saved by a high school drama teacher. The theater was his God. The rest was tripe.

I was counting up the day's dough and stuffing it into a pair of shoddy vinyl envelopes when I caught sight of Christian sauntering through the main floor. He was decked out in a gray flannel suit; a black raincoat hung carelessly over his forearm, its belt dragged along the floor behind him. He was stylishly messy in that peculiar European way. I prayed he'd turn around and spare me the embarrassment of running into him. But it was not to be.

"I was trying for you in the designer," he said, cheerfully.

I smiled as best I could. "You still found me."

"I am very thorough," he said. "Anyway, I was looking at some things."

"I don't see any things."

Christian shook his head. "I'm not much for the shopping today." He glanced at his watch. "When are you finished?"

"I was just about to leave."

"My timing is very nice."

I nodded. Maybe he'd buy me dinner. That'd be alright with me. I was sick of scrambled eggs. Before I could suggest it, Malcolm was on us like a hawk. "Hello," he said in a booming voice, shoving a hairy paw in front of Christian. "I'm Malcolm R. Foxman, *the playwright.*"

"I am Christian Olsen," Christian said, as Malcolm pumped his arm up and down. "I am a designer and architect."

"Christian's my neighbor," I said.

"How convenient," Malcolm said. "And I suppose you're from some quaint little socialist country where everyone is blond and blue-eyed and fit as a well-tuned fiddle." He pushed his thick glasses up the bridge of his nose and sized Christian up. "Do you design windmills?"

Christian shook his head. "I am from Sweden. You are thinking of the Holland."

"Ah, geography," Malcolm said. "Do you know my work?"

Malcolm was intent on toying with Christian. I tried to cut him off. "He couldn't possibly know your plays, Malcolm."

"I suppose," he sniffed. "Well, then, what about *Miss Julie?*"

Christian's eyes widened. "I am knowing the Strindberg very well," he said, nodding slowly. "He is famous in my country."

"I see," Malcolm said, disinterestedly. "Are you interested in Judeo pathology?"

Christian smiled. "I am interested in everything."

"Simon Wiesenthal, too?" Malcolm asked.

"What are you saying?" Christian said.

"Never mind," Malcolm said. "It was a pleasure to meet you. Really. Now away, you two. Out of my sight."

Christian took out his cigarettes. "I am going outside," he said, pointing to the exit. "I will wait for you."

"I'll be two minutes," I said.

Malcolm began to straighten, hovering over a table of socks.

"I already closed the registers," I said.

But Malcolm wasn't listening. "Malcolm?"

"I hope you did it right."

Like he gave a rat's ass.

"What are you looking at?" he said, glancing up from a pile of pink wool tights.

"Nothing," I said.

"Go to your Nazi."

"Zeig heil, kommandant."

He didn't laugh. "You don't want to be around me," he said. "I'm dismal, abysmal, cataclysmal."

"I'm sorry." I wasn't sure why I was apologizing.

"Toodles."

I gave him a light pat on the back and he started, as though I'd touched him with a hot iron. "Christ."

"It's all right," he said. "I really don't like to be touched."

"You read too much Beckett."

He shot me a quick smile. "Maybe I'll pick up a Harlequin Romance."

"That might help."

"Don't you worry about me."

"Don't worry, Malcolm," I said. "I don't."

• • •

Christian and I scooted back to the building. A fierce wind blew in our faces. He chatted the whole time about a friend who'd just moved to Pakistan to start an "import-export" company. Christian was vague about the details, and I tried to imagine what sort of things his friend was bringing into the country—bowls, saris, bombs, whatever—and how any of this would be of interest to an architect. But I kept my thoughts to myself. It sounded a little shady, and—again—I had a nagging suspicion that Christian wasn't playing straight with me. I also had the odd feeling—again—that we were being followed. I looked over my shoulder, trying not to be obvious, but no one was there. Carmi would've been pleased: I was a paranoid New Yorker in just over a week.

Surprisingly, Christian didn't ask me to have dinner with him. He didn't want to come in either. I was almost insulted. He apologized profusely, but he was in a hurry; he had an important business matter. He'd make it up to me, he said. I asked him what was so pressing. He was expecting a call from his friend—the one in Pakistan—about some stone he'd ordered for the kitchen of a condo on the Upper East Side. His client was "wanting the ethnic." I wished him luck and said good-bye.

I made myself a ham sandwich on a toasted bagel and read the *Times.* I added a few more things to my to-do list. Then I called my mother and chatted for an hour. She asked if I'd heard from Carmi and if I'd found a decent job. I told her I was working at Barneys—in the advertising department. I didn't want to let on that I was back to hustling clothes. She gave me the dirt on the rest of the family. The dirt wasn't very scandalous. We're a pretty predictable bunch.

chapter 9

When I returned from a walk around the block, there were two messages from Kyle—boyish apologies for abandoning me in his hovel. I deleted his scratchy voice. He was on my shit list. When the phone rang, I assumed it was Christian—changing his mind about taking me out. But it was Kyle again. I could barely hear him over the cacophonous voices in the background.

"I'm at the dive on the corner," he shouted.

"So?"

"C'mon, Alex. Don't be like that," he said, as though I was the difficult one. "I said I was sorry."

"I just got home."

"Come down."

"No," I said. "I don't feel like it."

"I'll buy you a beer," he said. "To make up for last night."

"Gee, thanks," I said. He made it sound like he was giving me a diamond.

"C'mon, don't be a baby," he pleaded. "I said I was sorry."

I didn't say anything.

"You'll be able to find your way home." He laughed.

"I'm not worried about that," I said. "I'm tired."

"You can sleep when you're dead."

He had a point. I listened to the commotion in the background. "Well?"

"Maybe," I said. I couldn't decide which was worse—hanging around with Kyle or sitting alone at Carmi's.

"Cool," he said. "It's the Irish bar on Nineteenth . . ."

"I know it."

"Later," he said. The phone went dead in my ear. I held the receiver for a minute trying to make up my mind. I had a feeling the elusive Yassi would be there. I was curious, if only because Kyle had told me so many tall tales about her. I knew what I was getting myself into. I was about to take part in one of Kyle's favorite scams: He'd drag me along somewhere to meet a woman he was trying to impress. The idea was I upped his cool quotient by about 50 percent. Kyle's rationale: If she's following me around, then I must have something going on, right? It was a tried-and-true plan that almost always got him laid, though you never could trust Kyle. Obviously, it didn't do much for me.

Kyle was stationed by the door like a sentry. As soon as he saw me, he pounced, pressing my face into the hollow of his rib cage. I didn't mind his rough-house affection; you got used to it after a while. He grabbed my wrist and led me past the packed bar to a corner booth, where a woman who I knew had to be Yassi sat with a pair of long legs jutting out, her arms wrapped around her shaved head like some exotic barfly Shiva. She had glassy eyes and a tiny pointy nose, almost Barbie doll–like. I had a feeling I'd seen her before, though I couldn't place where. Kyle slithered in beside her. Yassi wasn't surprised to see me. Her mouth remained straight as a ruler, a cigarette dangled between her chapped lips. She was Kyle's type—lank and serpentine, with the worn look of someone washed once too often.

"This is 'The Alex,'" Kyle announced.

Yassi nodded coolly. "He talks about you all the time."

I said my friendliest hello. Kyle abandoned us for the bar. For a minute, we didn't say anything. I raced through a bunch of possibilities. But she got there first.

"Kyle never told me you were pretty." Yassi narrowed her eyes. "Do you fuck him?"

"No."

"He says you did."

"He lies a lot."

"He's a fucker."

"Yeah." They usually said he was an asshole.

"Why are you friends with him?"

"I don't know," I said.

"He has a big cock."

Like I cared. "So he says."

She sighed, then bit at a thumbnail. Her fingers were chewed to the quick. "He can't keep it up."

"I'm not interested."

"I'm just telling you."

I noticed she didn't have much of an accent. "I thought you were French." That's what Kyle had said.

"I was born in Algeria. My parents are fundamentalists."

Just like Christian's girlfriend. Who knew there were so many Algerians in New York. It was hard to believe.

Kyle made his way back to us and slammed the beers on the table. He must have overheard my question because he blurted: "She's carried an Uzi." He looked at her respectfully. "Don't fuck with her."

I didn't believe him either, but I played along for the fun of it. "Were you in the army?" I asked.

Yassi grabbed a beer and threw herself against the back of her chair, pressing a combat boot into the table; she had little feet. "Sort of. It was more of a movement."

"She's a revolutionary," Kyle said, slipping his hand around her slender thigh. She shook him off with one harsh jerk. He made a face, grumbled something under his breath, and took off again with his beer.

"It was a movement, not a revolution." She took a long, greedy gulp. "Against the elitist bastards."

Now it was going to get interesting. "What elitist bastards?" I asked.

"All of them. Every last sucking one."

Yassi was by far the most "radical" of Kyle's women, although there'd once been a French *femme* who had a bad habit of smacking her head against a wall whenever Kyle derailed her. I wondered what Yassi might do if provoked. She seemed pretty upset already, her mouth turned down at the corners, her eyes clouded up with images of the dreaded elitists. As for me, I sympathized with her. I'd always had a soft spot for the hard-core idealists. The tree-huggers, the marchers, the wide-eyed, bushy-tailed coeds raging at the machine. But I'd never been a jump-on-the-bandwagon type. I was a believer, an empathizer, but not an organizer. With this in mind, I turned to Yassi and said: "I know what you mean."

She grinned. "You Americans are all so naive."

"It's true," I lied. "You'd be surprised. The circles I've traveled in." But she didn't seem to bite, or maybe she thought my routine was dumb. Whatever the reason, Yassi was back to frowning and scanning the bar, her fingers making a dum-dum noise on the table. I followed her sight line and found the real source of her black mood: Kyle was busy flirting with a giant red-haired woman in a black ski suit.

Suddenly, Yassi stood up, the chair scraping the floor beneath her. "I'm splitting." She scratched her forearm with a hand of ragged nails.

Kyle caught a glimpse of Yassi pulling on her hat; he left the Amazon and raced back to the table. "Where you flyin' off to?"

"Like you care," Yassi said.

"I do," Kyle said. "Tell her, Alex."

I opened my mouth then closed it.

"I'm late already," she said, looking at her watch. "I'm meeting someone."

"I want to come," Kyle said.

"I don't have money for you," she said.

He looked at me.

"Forget it," I said, inching toward the door.

"Come on," he said. "I hardly ever ask."

I shook my head. Bankrolling Kyle on my sock-and-hat change didn't rank high on my priorities.

"Come on," he said, again.

"No," I said. "I'm leaving, too."

Kyle frowned. He wasn't used to being deserted.

Yassi led the way, bumping into a table and ranting. Outside, a wet snow had begun to fall. I put on my gloves, my fingers already going cold. The street was quiet except for the occasional honk of a passing cab. I thought Kyle was right behind us. But he wasn't. Yassi lit a cigarette. Then she said, "Fuck him. You want to get high?" This was something new: a fundamentalist druggie. That was one way to get closer to God. I said I had to work tomorrow, even though it wasn't true. She looked me over again. "You really are pretty," she said.

"It's all the milk I drink."

She smiled. It changed her face. She looked five years younger. "I used to be. But now I'm worn out. Kyle says I look like a lizard."

I wanted to say he compared all his women to reptiles or insects. But I didn't want to ruin it for her.

"You sure you don't want to come?" Her eyes softened into gray pools; they were feline, flecked with dark imperfections.

"Some other time," I said. I didn't want to get to know her. I was afraid I might like her. I said good-night and headed back to Carmi's, leaving Yassi to smoke while giant wet flakes collected around her. I didn't bother waiting for Kyle. I'd gotten my free beer—his big apology. And I'd made him look good. What else were friends for?

When I got home, there was another message from Carmi saying that he was sorry he missed me. There was also an envelope lying on the floor. Someone had slipped it under the door. I thought it might be a note from the super, giving me the low-down on a leaky faucet. But it wasn't. On expensive ecru stationery embossed with his initials, Christian had written me a note. It said:

> Dear Alex,
> Dinner was pleasure for me. I wish you to accompany me for a shopping tour. I am needing to buy some things. Please answer yes and slip it under my door. I am taking you to lunche. Oh, the rendezvous is for Sunday noon.
> From your neighbor,
> Christian

I checked out the envelope, the paper, his curly girlish handwriting. His signature was a tangle of graceful lines. I'd never been asked out so formally. It was sort of charming. I found some paper and, without being too enthusiastic, accepted his weird invitation. I sneaked into the hallway and slipped it under his door, afraid for a moment that he was waiting on the other side. But his lights were out and his apartment was dead quiet. That night, I tossed and turned in Carmi's skinny bed, first thinking about Christian and then wondering what it'd be like to see Jan again.

chapter 10

Christian picked me up promptly at noon. He was tricked out in a crumpled brown suit with a pink Hermès tie and drenched in flowery cologne. His hair was slicked down and his skin scrubbed and shining. He looked like a nineteenth-century lord. During lunch, Christian explained that he liked to shop. He said his closets were stuffed with clothes and shoes, even though he claimed to wear the same thing every other day, which wasn't exactly true. I didn't argue with him. I could tell Christian liked cultivating what he thought was an eccentric persona.

Our odyssey began at an Italian boutique on Madison, where Christian scooped up half a dozen shoes and boots and saun-tered over to a massive tuck-and-roll leather couch. He lounged imperiously, the security guard eyeing him, waiting for a sales-person to notice.

"You're going to try all those on?" I asked.

"Yah," he said, patting me on the thigh. "Or how am I knowing what I am liking?"

He had a point.

Christian waved at a dwarfish saleswoman. She moped over and took his size. Ten minutes later she was back with a tower of boxes; he plowed right in, shoehorn in hand. Loafers and boots slid on and off like a conveyor belt.

"Are you liking these?" he asked. His wide feet pushing over the edges of a pair of two-tone patent-leather loafers with paper-thin soles. They were $425.

"Those aren't really you."

"Why?" he demanded, pointing a glossy toe at me.

"I don't know," I said. "They look like something you'd wear to the opera."

"We can go if you are wanting," he said, grinning like I'd invited him to *Rigoletto.*

"Get them then."

He stomped around the Persian rug, doing a few *tendus* in front of the mirror. "I will take them," he said to the shriveled woman. "I will pay cash." Christian pulled out a wallet that was stuffed with crisp hundred dollar bills. I remember thinking he must've been paid off the books at the architectural firm, being European and all.

"Nothing for you?" she said, eyeing me from behind bifocals.

"Not today," I said. I got a discount at Barneys.

"Why not?" said Christian, padding over to the women's shoes in his socks. "What about this?" He held up a dark red stiletto. "No, thanks," I said. "Too uncomfortable." And too cheesy.

He let out a high-pitched giggle, stuck a loafer and a pump under each arm, and sauntered back to the couch.

"Here," he said to the saleswoman. "She will try."

"No," I said. "Really. I won't try."

"Yes. She will try," he said, ignoring me. "Bring size thirty-seven or thirty-eight." He shooed her away with a flick of his wrist.

"How'd you know I wear a seven?" I said, impressed by his perceptiveness.

"Your feet are looking average," he said, glancing at them.

I wondered what "average" feet looked like. "You do this a lot?" I said.

"What I am doing?" he replied, a note of concern in his voice.

"This thing."

"I am not doing any thing."

I shook my head; he was refusing to understand, talking in circles.

I slipped on the shiny black pumps; they had narrow inverted heels. Christian's lower lip quivered slightly. He kept saying how nice they looked on me. I took a spin around the boutique. In the mirror, my calves looked longer than they actually were. I didn't have long legs, but they were slender and decently shaped. The shoes did look nice.

"You are liking?" he asked, his eyes glowing.

"I am liking."

"You are looking sexy."

I smiled. They were lovely shoes.

"You will wear them today," he said.

"I'm not getting them."

"I will buy."

"Don't be ridiculous."

"You will allow me to buy," he said. "Or I am insulted."

"Then be insulted."

The high-pitched chirp of his cell phone interrupted us. Christian blushed, lifted a finger, and took the call. He moved away from me so I couldn't hear what he was saying. A salesperson walked by and complimented my taste.

When he returned, Christian went on to list a dozen reasons why it was okay for him to buy me shoes. I shook my head. I said no about a hundred times. But he would not be discouraged. He was having a ball. I slipped off the pumps and tossed them in the box. Shriveled Woman smirked to herself. She probably thought I was Christian's mistress.

"I'll be outside," I said, shoving my arms into my parka.

"You are insulting me," he said, a fake pout on his face.

"Don't take it so hard," I said, leaving Christian in the shop.

A few minutes later, he sauntered out swinging two bags.

"These are for you," he said. "From me. Please do not refuse. Please do not say anything." He reached out and lightly touched my lips with the back of his index finger. It was sort of poignant.

As I took the bag from his hand, he said: "Ruin them, if you are wanting." For the moment, I didn't say anything. Arguing with Christian on the sidewalk would only cause a scene. I'd return the shoes later. The rest of the afternoon I followed Christian from store to store. He bought a lot of things for himself, but didn't offer to buy anything else for me. It was a relief.

chapter 11

The next morning, Malcolm was gabbing loudly with his agent on the phone, punctuating every statement with a karate chop in the air. The floor had been entirely rearranged. He'd probably come in early and redone the place. There were floppy straw hats, polka-dot bathing suits, and canvas tote bags. It was resort time for the jet set. I fantasized about basking in the sun on some sultry Caribbean island. I hadn't made it to the water before Malcolm slammed down the phone, reminding me of where I was. He didn't say good-morning.

"Good-morning, Malcolm," I said, loudly.

"What's good about it?" He frowned like he'd just sucked on a lemon.

"Nothing yet." I should have greeted him with an insult; he probably would've preferred it. He hated phony civility.

He peered over his glasses. "Well?"

"Well, what?"

"Did you *read* it?" He practically yelped.

"Read what?" Then it dawned on me: his play.

"My fucking opus, my masterpiece."

His play. I'd read the first act, fallen asleep, and spent ten minutes this morning reorganizing the pages that had spilled all over the floor. I said: "Of course, I read it." I didn't sound very convincing.

That was Malcolm's cue. "You didn't read it at all."

"I did so. I read the first act."

"That's like taking a sip of Dom Perignon and throwing the rest away."

"Don't you think you're overreacting?"

He let out an irritated humph and shook his head. "You were too busy canoodling with your Nazi."

"Busy walking home. "

"I don't believe you."

"I don't care."

"You wouldn't." He scrunched up his face. Then he slammed a few cabinet doors for emphasis. I guess we were having a fight.

"Cute always wins," he said.

"What are you talking about?"

"The Nazi."

"What about him?"

"He's cute."

"So what."

"I bet you get all the cute ones. Like a magnet you are."

Right. He should meet Kyle.

"That's why you don't care about me. You have all these boys flocking round you like sheep, swinging their gigantic members like divining rods."

"How ridiculous you are."

"You didn't read it."

"I told you," I said. "I read the first act."

"That's not good enough," he shouted, his voice cracking. People turned their heads. I was mortified.

"That's it," he said, taking out his cigarettes. "It's over."

Were we breaking up? Had we ever been together? I'd read the first act of his silly, goddamn play and even liked it. That was more than most people would've done.

"You just don't understand what it's like," he said, still shrieking, his hand on the glass door. "To slave away in obscurity, in the dark. Alone day in and day out. No one to support you. No one around to even ask what it is you're trying to do."

He looked like he was about to start sobbing—not that it would've been genuine. All that was missing were the violins. Still, I was beginning to feel shittier by the minute.

"This is so incredible," he said, a note of accusation in his voice. "And from you . . . of all people."

"I'm sorry," I said. "I really am."

"Don't," he said, raising his hand like a stop sign. "Just do me the favor of bringing it back. It's my only copy."

With that, he slammed the door so hard the windows shook. Everyone was watching. The queens in the shoe department were snickering behind their palms. Customers hurried out of the CO/OP—there went today's bread. When I caught his eye, the security guard shrugged. He'd probably seen it all before. Malcolm thought he was on stage, a perpetual dramatist. I slunk back to the counter and pretended to look for something in my purse.

Malcolm didn't come back for two hours. I told Olga he was in the bathroom, sick with diarrhea. She almost believed me. When he finally did show up, he stalked across the floor like a madman, stinking of cigarettes. He gave me the silent treatment for the rest of the afternoon. When he had to communicate with me, he sent the anorexic diva from the lingerie department to deliver his message. She loved it. Any shard of gossip was cause for celebration. Pretty soon the whole store knew that the "Iranian-looking bitch in the CO/OP dissed Malcolm's play."

When my shift finally inched to a close, I flew out of there without a word to Malcolm. He'd pushed his luck a little too far. Trudging back to Carmi's, it dawned on me that I'd never had a normal friendship. They were always a series of sick trial-and-error schemes. I was the one who had to work at giving them normalcy. It was becoming tedious.

When I got home, there was a message from Christian. Would I please meet him at his gym tomorrow? He was "wanting to show me how to work out." There was no need to call back.

As far as Christian was concerned, I couldn't possibly say no. Of course, I could've said no—I probably should've since Jan would be here in a few days. But I didn't.

While eating Chinese takeout, I finished Malcolm's play. It was about a man named Peter Piper who's driven mad by his doting mother. After a harrowing escape from an asylum, Peter wrecks havoc on his family with a band of misanthropic angels. It was pure Malcolm—an obsessive ode to the two pivotal moments in his life: birth and circumcision. He was talented, but it was a small talent. Still, it made me laugh.

chapter 12

Christian showed up ten minutes late with a lit cigarette and a steaming cup of coffee. His right eye was slightly swollen, his forehead scratched. When I asked him what happened, he started jabbering about the soirée he'd attended the previous evening. "A friend," he said, "was having the party." As it turned out, things got slightly out of hand. Christian didn't seem too upset. He said it was like being in "the American movie." I reminded him that this was real life. But he only laughed and said I worried too much. I'd never known anyone to get punched at a party. It sounded fishy. Maybe I'd never been to *that* kind of party.

I followed Christian into the gym's inner sanctum, a slick three-level club with an outrageous membership fee, or so he told me. On a weekday midmorning, it wasn't very crowded. "There is the women's change room." He pointed to a corridor. "I will meet you here. After you are changed."

I nodded. I could hardly hear him over the din of pounding disco.

As I trudged to the locker room it occurred to me that I didn't really want to work out. I guess I just wanted to see Christian again. Hard as it was to admit, I sort of liked him.

When I saw Christian, I almost laughed out loud. He was swathed in tight red shorts and a tank top that was too small; his sneakers looked like space shoes. Sweatbands were carefully positioned on his wrists and head; a towel was draped round his neck. All he needed was a whistle and he could've been a cruise-ship aerobics instructor. "You are ready?" he said.

"Ready as I'll ever be."

He guided me to the first contraption, trying to check out my exercise getup—sports bra and tight shorts—without being too obvious. "This will work out the gluteus," he said. All around us people grunted and groaned. "It is very good for the women."

"I see," I said. My behind was certainly a work in progress.

"I will show," he said. He set his blue energy drink next to the machine and lay face down on the bench, his golden hair catching the light. He slid his ankles under the weights and yanked them toward the ceiling, his butt cheeks clenching like fists. He repeated this about ten times, exhaling loudly through the mouth. Then he jumped off the bench, red-faced, rivulets of perspiration dampening his hairline. "Now you," he said, smiling.

I slid on while he adjusted the weights. "Make it light," I said.

"Okay," he said. "Go. Now."

I felt like a horse at the gate. "Go!" he said. I lifted my legs. The weight resisted like a determined sack of spuds.

"Good," he said. "You are stronger than most girls." He giggled.

I did it four more times. "Okay," I said. "I'm done." My legs weighed eighty pounds; I was thirsty.

"No," he said. "You must do five more to make ten. You need to be regimen." He scurried in front of me and bent down to my eye level. I had one cheek resting on the sticky cushion. "Just five more. You must."

"Must I?" I said, amused that Christian was so serious about his workouts. I had a vision of a Volvo factory filled with Christian's cousins. They were all toned, blond, and buff from a diet of pickled herring and tiny meatballs. "Okay," I said. "Count for me."

He smiled and patted me on the head. He counted each repetition, capping the set with a triumphant "Ten!"

We kept at it for about an hour, rotating around the room until Christian was covered in a film of sweat and I was numb. Christian talked about body fat, nutrition, Power Bars. For all his working out, he should've looked more like Charles Atlas than an overly indulged, baby-fatted European. When I asked him why he smoked, he said he didn't—it was just for show. While I waited for him to finish a set of bench presses, I watched a couple of really fit women climb their StairMasters. I thought they were very determined.

"Come," he said, mopping his forehead with a towel. "We will relax now."

It sounded like the first good idea of the day. I followed him past the lockers down a long, dimly lit corridor toward a door with a sign that read MEN'S STEAM ROOM. Christian slipped in before I could say anything. He immediately came out, his face wild with excitement. "It's okay," he said, his eyes shining. He started pulling off his shirt in the hallway. "Yah," he said, more to himself than to me. "It's okay."

"What's okay?"

He squealed. "It's okay. I know a trick," he said. He pulled the sign from its plastic shield and replaced it with another from his bag. The new sign read TEMPORARILY CLOSED FOR CLEANING. SORRY FOR THE INCONVEENANCE. The word "inconvenience" was misspelled.

"Come," he said. "Faster." He was naked except for his shorts. His stomach crept over the elastic like butter cream on a cake. I looked down the corridor, terrified that someone might see us. I hated clandestine operations.

"Stop fooling around," I said.

"Please," he said. "I will be a good boy." He laughed, pulling the door open and pecking my nose as a cloud of steam brushed our faces. He said something exasperated in Swedish, grabbed a towel, and let the door go. It slammed shut. I stood in the corridor by myself, Christian's gym bag stuffed into the towel closet. Maybe he was right. Maybe I was acting like a prude. I stood another moment with my hand on the door. I didn't like to think I was incapable of railing against my proper Catholic upbringing. I wrapped a towel around my waist and gave the door a yank. I could barely see Christian splayed on a redwood bench, arms above his head, belly protruding. I stepped on his red shorts, a bright wad on the floor.

He sat up, his skin the color of pomegranates. "You are wearing your top?"

"Did you think I'd strip in the hall?"

He giggled. "But you are undressing?"

"I'm undressing," I said.

"You will be naked?"

"Yes," I said. "When I take off my clothes."

He smiled at the idea.

"Turn around or something."

"I am closing my eyes."

I turned my back and wiggled out of my clothes.

"All right," I said, stretching out on a bench and untangling my hair. "I'm done."

Christian abruptly sat up. "But the towel," he said. "You are not naked."

"You're not naked either." He had a towel torqued around his waist.

He considered the facts for a moment, then settled back into his bench. The steam hissed through invisible holes, filling up the tiny room. The redwood was hot underneath me. Soon I was drifting off. Christian was saying something but I wasn't listening. I was almost asleep when I felt his hand lightly brushing my thigh. I let him; it felt good. "What if someone comes in?" I asked.

"It is okay," he whispered. "No one is coming." He moved closer to me; I could feel his breath. "You are sexy," he said, risking a kiss on my shoulder. His lips felt like a caterpillar on my skin.

"You better stop," I said.

"Why?" he said, continuing along my arm. "We are only getting to be friends." He kept at it. His palms dragging around my shoulder. He stroked my neck for a while. I hardly felt my body. That is until Christian jerked open my towel and tweaked my breast. I almost fell off the bench. "Jesus," I said, batting his hand away and covering myself. "Not in here."

"Why?" he said. "You are not liking?"

I sat up. I was awake now. Christian's face was completely flushed, beads of perspiration clustered on his forehead. His towel was pointing at me like an arrow. He laid his hands on his lap, trying to hide the evidence, and waited for me to say something. He looked almost cherubic, like a face you'd find on a Victorian Valentine's Day card. I leaned over and kissed him gently. He smiled a dizzyingly pretty if confused smile.

"I think we should go," I said.

He shut his eyes. "No," he said. "Not yet. Kiss me again."

I kissed him again.

"Just a little more," he said. "Please."

"No more," I said. "At least not in here."

This encouraged him. He picked up his gym shorts and shook them out. "It is what you want," he said. I turned my back so he could struggle with his shorts in private. I slipped out the door, towel wrapped tightly around me, and bolted to the locker room. In a public sauna of all places, with a silly, fatted Swede. I really must have been desperate. I took a freezing shower and changed into my street clothes.

Christian was waiting for me in the lobby, a smile pasted on his face as if nothing had happened. We went out for steak frites and chocolate mousse, drank a lot of expensive burgundy, and smoked a pack of cigarettes. I guess we were both frustrated.

When we got back to the apartment, I invited him in. Nothing happened. We were both beached whales. Christian hit the caffeine train while I dipped into Carmi's amaretto. He sipped cup after cup of black coffee, rambling on about his lonely childhood. He'd been shipped off to boarding schools in Switzerland; he'd had a very moral upbringing, but he'd always been naughty. In his teens, he'd spent a lot of time in Amsterdam smoking hash and wandering around the Red Light district. He'd been afraid of sex until the family housekeeper, an Albanian woman who barely spoke Swedish, "took advantage" of him. He still dreamed of her. She was his first love and, even now, when he went back to Sweden, she still made him cocoa the way he liked it. Not too sweet. But they no longer slept together. "She's too old," he said. "It would be like making love to Mama."

I could picture Christian as a shy, slight sixteen-year-old. The idea somehow endeared him to me. That evening, we had a lot in common. We both felt it. I could tell by the way he looked at me before I kicked him out, like I was condemning him to a life of solitary confinement. But what was the alternative? We couldn't possibly spend the night together because spending the night might actually mean something more—something I wasn't willing to risk.

chapter 13

I'd forgotten Malcolm's play—again. I was picking up a cup of bad coffee at a dive near Barneys when it dawned on me. I cursed and glanced at my watch—it was too late to run home and get it. The streets were slick with ice, snow flurries twisted and turned in the air. I wasn't going to trudge all the way back home on Malcolm's account. He probably wasn't speaking to me. Now he'd really have something to sulk about.

When I rolled in, Malcolm was already on the floor, whistling and doing his usual walkabout routine. He was surprisingly chipper, greeting me with a sing-song "Good-morning" that caught me off guard.

"Feeling better, princess?" he said, furiously refolding a stack of floral neckerchiefs.

"Yes," I said, surprised that he'd deigned to speak to me. "Thanks."

"Did your Nazi attend to you?"

"No," I said. "And he's not a Nazi." I was sick to death of the Nazi thing.

"That's what they all say." He gave me a wink. I waited for more, but nothing came. I thought I'd test the waters. "I read your play."

"About time," he said, quietly, his hands still for a minute.

"I thought it was smart," I said. "And very funny."

"What did you expect?"

"Nothing short of genius." I was laying it on thick now. For once, Malcolm seemed at a loss for words.

"Well," he said, picking up a handful of crocheted scarves. "Plans have changed. Genius will have to wait."

I almost asked if he was feeling okay. "You're throwing in the towel?"

"Oh, heavens no," he said. "I've decided to become a *commercial* writer. I've sold out to the almighty dollar and I couldn't be happier to leave this stinking hen house." He stomped his foot for emphasis.

"Translation?"

"I'm writing for the boob tube."

"Oh."

He shrugged. "It's just cops-and-robbers nonsense. Big men with guns. Zero kink. I do have a contract though. You can express your interest through my agent."

"So," I said. "You're out of here?"

"Not right away," he said. "But they did give me something up front. It's not enough for foie gras and claret."

"It's a start."

"I suppose," he said with a sigh. "All great artists have to suffer at some point."

I laughed. Even if he had his own prime-time special, Malcolm would always suffer. "How'd the TV people find you?"

He looked at me as though the answer was obvious. "I have a gift for violence. You should know this from your reading."

"Yes," I said. "Tofu Jackson comes to a very bad end."

Malcolm adopted a thoughtful air. "Death is so liberating. But untimely death is . . . downright tragic. That's how I want to go," he continued. "I want everyone to cry about my premature demise. *'Merde,'* they'll say. 'He was such a vibrant youth!' Then they'll serve course after course of exotic hors d'oeuvres." He shook his hairy fist. "'What a spiteful bastard God can be, with his asinine ways!'" He was quoting one of his characters. It was quite a performance.

A woman in her forties asked if she could get some help. Malcolm spotted her Hermès bag and canned the dramatic reverie. In a flash, he was on her, oozing semi-ironic obsequiousness. She lapped it up while he sold her the priciest stuff he could find. He was nothing short of amazing.

I couldn't get over his mood; he'd forgotten the insult. I had a feeling this happened a lot—pitching fits and making scenes only to forget them as soon as something more interesting arrived. In this case, it was a few bucks and a lot of blown smoke. That was all right with me. I liked Malcolm the best when he was on top of the world.

Around eleven that night, the doorbell rang. I was already in my robe. Through the peephole, I saw Christian swinging his battered leather briefcase back and forth. I thought about ignoring him. But Jan would be here tomorrow. I had to tell Christian he couldn't keep dropping in.

He was already tossed, his face blotchy, eyelids puffy. His shirttail draped over his wrinkled trousers, a button hung by a single thread from his jacket. But his shoes were brand new, buffed to a deep brown glow. He didn't smile at me. Instead, he shoved a bottle of wine into my hands and gave me a quick peck on each cheek. He threw himself on the couch.

"You will give me some wine," he said, rubbing his face.

"I guess I have no choice," I said, uncorking the merlot in the kitchen. Christian didn't bother saying cheers, or whatever they said in Sweden. He gulped down the vino and refilled his glass.

"What's the matter with you?"

"My old girlfriend, Giti, has to stay on my apartment for a few days," he said. "I cannot come to you."

I almost asked why she *had* to. But it didn't matter. "Jan will be here tomorrow, too," I said.

He looked hurt. "I forgot about him."

"I didn't."

Christian downed his wine and refilled his glass again. "I am not liking to be controlled."

"It's only a temporary arrangement."

Christian didn't brighten up. "I am not loving her."

I wanted to ask him why he let her stay with him. But there wasn't any point. Then I'd have to ask myself why I was seeing Jan. I was pretty sure I was "not loving him" either, not at the moment anyhow. It was the end for Christian and me. We both knew it.

"This is what you call really bad timing," I said.

He nodded, his face still the picture of dejection. I was sort of touched. He really did want to keep "coming to me." It was sweet in the most artificial of ways. "Yes," he said, standing up, a dribble of red wine running down his shirtfront like blood. He absently rubbed the stain with his finger. "It is too bad for me," he said.

Christian's phone started ringing inside his briefcase. "My cell," he said, excitedly, plucking it from an outside pocket like a truffle hound. "Yah," he said. "This is Christian." He raised his finger again and sauntered boldly into Carmi's bedroom with his briefcase in hand. I couldn't understand why he needed privacy; he was speaking something that sounded more like Hebrew than Swedish.

Two minutes later he was back, sitting next to me. When I asked what language he'd been babbling, he said, "Arabic." I was impressed. "I am only knowing it a little," he said. "I learned it in the Berlitz." Then, before I could ask what he was talking about, he reached across me to switch off the lamp. "It is too much on my eyes," he said, slipping his arm around me and planting one on my lips. He tasted like wine, his tongue darting around in my mouth like a ripe grape. Tonight I found Christian sort of exciting. Maybe it was all the unfulfilled foreplay. He had me pinned to the couch, his crotch digging into my inner thigh. He flayed around as though overcome with passion. It was almost comical. Soon he was fumbling with the belt on my robe. Then he was burying his face in my breasts, his forehead sweaty on my skin. He spent a lot of time fondling and suckling like a pup. I wasn't thinking about anything. Somehow he managed to squirm out of his shirt, his white belly glowing. I stroked his back, his shoulders. He had nice skin. He murmured in another language. I didn't want to understand him. He rolled on his elbow to unbuckle his pants.

While Christian fiddled with his belt, Jan crossed my mind. I reached above our heads and switched on the lamp. Christian squinted into the bright light; his cheeks were flaming.

"What you are doing?"

"I'm sorry." I felt like a tease. "I can't."

"You are acting silly," he said, snapping off the light again. "Stop being so strict." He started kissing me again, sloppily, as though he wasn't thinking about me anymore. He probably wasn't. Maybe he never had been. I wasn't sure I could go through with it. I squeezed Jan out of my mind. Then, oddly, Kyle popped in for a visit. I could see him laughing at me. The whole thing was absurd. I gave Christian another gentle push.

"Christian," I said. "Forget it."

"Why?" he whined.

"I'm not in the mood."

"But you are liking it," he said, quickly sliding his hand between my legs and letting a finger trace the damp crotch of my panties. "I can tell."

"I am liking it," I said, smacking his hand. "It's not you."

"Why do you push me away?"

"I don't know."

"You are thinking about that Belgian."

I didn't say anything. It was obvious.

"He cannot find out," he said, tilting his head like a punished child, a few curls plastered to his brow. "I will not tell him."

"But I'll know," I said.

Christian nuzzled up to me again. "I am wanting to have you," he said, kissing me gently and pressing my hand into his crotch.

"Christian, this is silly."

"Why?" he asked, his voice straining. "We are good friends, no?"

"The very best."

"You always have sarcasm for me."

"I'm not being sarcastic."

He sighed, resigned to the fact that the evening was over. He sat up and swept his shirt off the floor.

"I guess I am going," he said. He poured the rest of the wine down his throat. He didn't bother with a glass.

I felt dismal.

He stood in the foyer. "I will not come to you for a while."

"I know."

"I will be missing you."

"I'll miss you, too."

"How long will he be in New York?"

"I'm not sure." Jan hadn't told me exactly how long he'd be staying.

Christian forced a smile. "Good-night."

"Good-night."

He gave me a rough one on my mouth. A last-ditch effort. The next thing I knew we were on the foyer floor. Christian was fumbling around with a rubber. He was from the fast-and-furious school, a quick pumper with a nice round butt to hold on to. It was a good, sweaty screw. We groped at each other and made a lot of noise. He got off before me, which didn't surprise me.

But I still managed, probably because I hadn't been with anyone in months. It was over in a heartbeat. And to think I'd made such a big deal about doing it in the first place. After that, Christian was in a much better mood. He stayed for another hour or so. We polished off Carmi's amaretto and chatted about nothing. Christian wanted to do it again but he was too bombed. We laughed it off and said next time. And that was it. I crawled in bed and slept like a log for the first time in months.

chapter 14

I spent two hours in the international terminal waiting for Jan's flight. I picked up a newspaper and settled into one of those greasy airport saloons where they sell skinny tasteless hot dogs and giant salty pretzels. It stunk of cigarette smoke and I joined right in, poisoning myself with bad coffee. Last night's adventure was still guiltily on my mind. I wondered if Christian had thought of me since; I hadn't heard a peep from him all day. Romping with Christian made me question what I'd felt about Jan in the first place. Jan and I had never said anything about fidelity, but my timing was shitty. I felt bad about it. I stuck my head back into the paper and tried to banish the thought from my head. It didn't take long for someone to realize I wasn't reading.

"Anyone sitting here?"

I looked up. He was a bit taller than me, dressed in a black suit and gray shirt sans tie. "No."

He yanked the chair noisily out from under the table and sat down. He stared at the crowd. "Come here often?"

I shook my head. I smiled. It was a pretty good line. "You?"

"I'm afraid so."

I took in his eyes: They were small, dark, and intelligent. I pretended to read again. I wasn't looking for a chat. Another time, I might've felt differently. A few minutes passed. I could hear Muzak tinkling somewhere.

He took a black spiral notebook from his jacket pocket and flipped through it. He seemed to be studying something. The arrival of Air India flight 907 was announced.

"Ever been there?" he asked.

"Where?"

"India."

"No."

"Real armpit."

"That so?"

He nodded. I wanted to ask what had brought him to such an armpit. But he was deep into his notebook, jotting something down. I went back to the paper. I could hear the rhythm of his tapping foot. Up and down. Up and down. The same beat. It sounded less nervous than expectant. I was about to ask him why he was here; then I realized I didn't want the question put to me. I folded up my newspaper.

"Leaving?"

"Checking on a flight."

"It'll be late," he said, still busy with his notebook.

"You don't even know what I'm checking."

"Only two birds comin' in at this hour. One from Islamabad, the other from Calcutta." He unbuttoned his jacket. "They're always late."

Jan was on Air India.

"By the way," he said, "my name's Jacob."

I smiled and said the first thing that crossed my mind. "I'm Candy."

"Candy?" He smiled. "No shit?" He cracked an ice cube between his teeth. I should've said Joan or something. He stared at me for a moment, his dark eyes on mine.

"You from the city?"

"Yeah."

"Where abouts?"

"Seventh and Fourteenth." I hadn't wanted to answer him but my mouth seemed to move independently. I had the unfortunate habit of being polite. I didn't know how to simply say fuck off—I really couldn't work up the nerve.

He moved his head slowly up and down as though he was trying to lay out a plan of attack.

"Listen," he said, quickly. "I want to invite you to a party. I'm a promoter and I give a lot of parties. He shoved his hand into his front pocket and produced a card: JACOB BLOOM, PROMOTER. There were four phone numbers listed.

"You have a lot of numbers," I said, taking the card from him. He had nice hands with shiny manicured nails.

He shrugged. "I'm hard to reach."

"I guess," I said, sliding off my chair.

"Thanks for the seat."

"Don't mention it."

"See you around."

"Bye."

I wandered down the concourse to have a look at the arrival monitor. The party promoter was wrong. The flight was on time. Jan would be here in five minutes; I felt nauseous. The moment had arrived. Now I wished I could take it back.

I watched as passengers streamed out of the jetway: Glassy, sleep-starved eyes roamed over the meet-and-greets. Most of the men were in white turbans; the women cocooned in saris as colorful as mosaics. Reunions commenced around me; people kissed and tweaked each another. I saw Jan before he saw me. His face was as striking as I remembered it. He had pallid skin set off by milky blue eyes and carnation pink lips. He was at least six four but seemed taller. I was transfixed; stuck to the linoleum beneath me. We stood there looking at each other for what seemed like ten minutes. Then he smiled and gave me a firm hug.

"I missed you," he said, still holding me. It felt as though we'd been apart for just a week, so I repeated the same thing back to him.

"Twenty hours," he said. "I wasn't sure you'd be here."

I'd never considered not showing up. "I wasn't sure *you'd* be here."

I took in his eyes again. They were different from any pair I'd ever seen—like saucers, almost transparent, a nonexistent shade of blue.

I stepped back and almost stumbled into Jacob, the party promoter. We made eye contact but he looked straight through me. I turned back to Jan. "Do you have any luggage?" I asked.

He shook his head. "Only this." He hoisted a small black suitcase in front of me.

"You travel light," I said.

"Always," he said. Jan gave off the aura of someone who could jump continents as though he were playing hopscotch.

While we headed down the escalator toward the idling cabs outside, I kept sneaking glances at him. He was as I remembered him—maybe his hair was darker, or the hollows of his cheeks were deeper. And he seemed to have gained a few pounds. When I told him so, he only laughed, his angular face breaking into soft planes.

"I always forget how busy New York is," he said, taking in the chaos around him.

"You've been here before?" He hadn't mentioned it. Or maybe he had. We'd talked about so many things in Europe, and done so much, I could hardly recall every detail.

"Oh," he said, nonchalantly. "Too many times to count."

It was odd to think that Jan probably knew more about New York than I did. He could play tour guide. I liked the idea.

"I guess you can show me around."

"Happily," Jan said.

I hadn't remembered how well he spoke; his English was near perfect. He'd told me his grandfather was British. His accent was practically undetectable.

Outside the day was gray; clouds were ganging up in clumps that threatened icy rain. We joined the line of freezing travelers and waited our turn for a cab. I huddled up next to Jan. He lit a cigarette then gently squeezed my hand. His palm was warm and smooth.

"You're cold," he said.

"It's this weather."

"It's worse in March," he said. "The wind tears you in half."

I couldn't imagine it being much colder. And by March, I'd be back in California.

Before long we were tucked in the backseat of a cab tearing along the Grand Central. It was one of those old wrecks; the beat-up seats squawked and rattled all the way to Manhattan. Jan glanced my way a few times like he was about to kiss me, but he didn't. He petted my hand, as if touching me was exciting enough in itself. And it was. I didn't mind if he wanted to begin cautiously. Actually, I preferred it. I'd become so used to the opposite phenomena—halfway through dinner your average guy was already telling you he was a reformed dope addict or an emotional cripple. Jan's reticence suited me.

He told the cabby that we'd be making two stops. He'd drop me off. Then he'd go to his hotel and crash, if that was okay with me. He'd pick me up about eight. It wasn't like I'd made other plans. I went back to Carmi's and waited for him.

Jan showed up at eight with an armful of white tulips. Carmi didn't have any vases, so I had to improvise with an empty tea kettle. We headed down the block to a tiny French restaurant I'd passed a dozen times. Jan had been there on his last trip; he said it was good, if you liked cassoulet and all. We took a cozy corner table near the back. The place was done up in pinks and mauves. Even the plates were rose. White candles burned on every table.

A fireplace roared in the center of the room. Jan ordered a bottle of Bordeaux from a waiter with a bad comb-over and a skinny mustache. Then he inspected me from across the table. "How long has it been since I saw you?" he said.

"Months," I said.

"More like years."

We both laughed. It had been a long time, but I didn't feel awkward. I didn't think Jan did either. The waiter returned with the wine and uncorked it. We ordered.

When we were alone again, Jan said: "There's only one thing then."

"What?"

"To drink wine, of course," he said, smiling.

Jan had crooked teeth—an imperfection I found charming.

"To drinking wine," I said. We clanked our glasses together.

I let the Bordeaux linger in my mouth for a moment.

"Why were you in India?" I said.

"I was visiting a friend," he said, buttering a roll. "And buying."

"Jewelry, you mean."

"Yes," he said. "The usual."

It wasn't the usual. People didn't trek halfway across the world to shop for jewelry. "There's nothing usual about it."

"You're right," Jan said. "It's serious work. Money. Gems. Poppadum. The Ganges. Elephants." The waiter set down our dinner.

"Did you ride around on one?" I said, picturing his skinny legs flanking leathery skin.

"An elephant?" Jan laughed. "Not exactly." He took a bite of cassoulet.

"My friend did though," he continued. "He's into that kind of thing."

"What kind of thing?"

"Riding elephants. Doing nothing on a beach in Goa. I'm jealous of him." Jan smiled. "We should go sometime. . . ." he said.

We'd barely finished a date and he was talking about traveling to a destination straight out of the Lonely Planet guide. I was flattered, but I was only just getting used to New York.

"Impractical," I said, though I could see myself going back to Europe for a while with Jan. It would be easy.

"I suppose," he said. "We hardly know each other."

I nodded. He was right.

"What I know," he said, his voice hesitant, "I like."

"Me, too," I said. That much was true. I did like Jan—he was different, from his eyes to the way his mind ticked along. Jan could be whimsical when he wanted to. He could propose something just as suddenly as he could abandon it.

Jan positioned his silverware at the ten and four o'clock marks on his plate. He had better manners than most women I knew. It was another thing about him I found charming.

When we finally stumbled out of the restaurant, the street was practically empty. We walked slowly back to Carmi's, stopping to admire a facade or look in a store window. We didn't talk about anything in particular—just everyday stuff, trivia about my job, what I'd been doing with myself in New York. It was effortless. I was glad he was there.

When we reached Carmi's building, I hesitated. I wasn't sure if I should invite him upstairs. I was on the verge when Christian pulled up in a cab. He rolled out—hair tossed every which way, face red and splotchy—and gave me a huge grin. He planted himself so close I could smell his syrupy cologne over the crisp night air. He gave Jan the once-over, giggled like a jackal, and said hello. I was forced to introduce him.

Jan shook his hand without much interest. Christian smiled and was off and running about Sweden and Belgium and how they were both quaint socialist countries. He'd been out to "meet some friend" to "celebrate the project." Eventually, he ran out of blather. He tried to catch my eye but I wouldn't let him. A silence fell upon us. Christian must've got the hint because he said a cheery good-night and traipsed into the building.

Once he was gone, Jan said: "Who was that annoying man?"

"He lives next door."

"You know him?"

"Not really," I said. "My uncle knows him."

"I don't think I like him."

"Why not?"

"He's an arrogant Dutchman," Jan said. He winked at me then turned to hail a cab.

"No," I said. "He's an arrogant Swede."

A cab pulled up. Jan kissed me in a way that made me want to ask him to stay. He lingered so long it seemed like he felt the same way. But Jan was too polite to invite himself. Before he slid across the seat, he said he'd call me. Then he was gone. I hung around for a minute—sort of stunned—watching the cars pass and generally feeling like I'd been swept off my feet.

chapter 15

The next evening we met for a late-night drink. Jan picked me up wearing a black turtleneck and jeans. His hair was carefully slicked back; his face clean-shaven. He looked like a handsome grad student on his way to a lecture. We'd wanted to go downtown but it was too bitter to walk and we couldn't get a cab. We ended up in a neighborhood joint with a massive wood bar, tall stools, and a mosaic floor. Christian had once recommended the place. It was cozy and half empty. And best of all, Christian was nowhere to be seen.

A waitress with hoops stuck through her crusty eyebrows asked us what we wanted. Jan made her rattle off all the American beers. He ordered a Rolling Rock; he wanted something authentic.

"I meant to tell you," Jan said, pausing with an unlit cigarette in his hand. "I met your Swedish neighbor in the lobby tonight."

"Christian?"

Jan nodded. "He was getting his mail."

"Did you talk to him?" I said.

"Of course," he said. "He told me about a renovation that he was working on."

"Oh," I said, thinking Christian was a little too friendly for my comfort. "He's an architect."

"I thought so," Jan said, taking a sip of his beer and making a face. "It's like water."

"The beer?"

He smiled. "I always forget."

"What else did he say?" I wanted the whole story.

"Not much," Jan said. "Just that he wanted to buy me a drink."

"What for?" I said. Christian's angelic face flashed across my consciousness. I wondered what he was up to.

"I don't know," Jan said. "But if he wants to buy me drink, I guess I'll let him."

"I thought you didn't like him."

"He's okay," Jan said, smiling. "I think he likes me. But it's a free country." He laughed at himself. He seemed to be in unusually high spirits, or maybe it was the booze.

I laughed, too, if only to appear natural. I wondered if I really knew Christian at all.

We were knocking back our second round when—to my surprise and dismay—Kyle burst through the door like a dervish. What the hell was he doing here? I had the feeling that Kyle had taken up stalking. He almost crushed a skinny girl lolling around the entranceway. She caught her balance and gave him a crooked smile. Kyle smiled back and devoured her lacy black slip dress. Then he leaned a pointy hip against a stool and gave the place a quick scan. I tried to hide behind Jan, but Kyle saw me. He waved as though he'd expected to run into me here.

He made his way toward us. "Hey," he said, thrusting a thumb toward the bar. "I think she wants me."

It was typical Kyle. He wasn't anyone until someone wanted him. I said: "Maybe you should tell her dad." I gave him a get-lost look. But Kyle only laughed.

For the second time, I was forced to introduce Jan to someone I didn't want him to know. I felt embarrassed introducing Kyle as my "oldest friend." But there wasn't any way around it and I was certainly used to it. I couldn't deny him—or the past eleven years. Jan didn't seem ruffled by the intrusion. He gave Kyle his best handshake.

"Belgium, right?" Kyle said.

"Yeah," Jan said. "You know, the country that invented the waffle."

"I lived with a Belgian chick in San Francisco," Kyle said, missing Jan's joke. "She was a juggler."

Jan smiled. I felt bad for him. He probably didn't know what to make of Kyle, though he seemed amused. He was still smiling.

The waitress came by to round up our empties. Jan ordered whisky, much to Kyle's delight. They were actually hitting it off. I could never have imagined them together.

"Yassi's split for good," Kyle said. "She stuck me with the rent on that rat hole."

"You'll get over it," I said. I gave Jan the lowdown on their doomed affair.

Kyle shook his head as though the depths of his sorrow were beyond me. I almost got out a tissue. "She's the woman I love, the woman I'd die for."

Kyle gave Slip Girl a big shit-eating grin. She smiled back.

"You'll live," Jan said, observantly. "Besides, you might meet another Belgian juggler."

Kyle's eyes lit up. "That would be cool."

Jan probably didn't care too much about Kyle's sloppy affairs. At the moment, neither did I. I wanted to get rid of him as soon as possible.

"Maybe you'll find this Yassi," Jan said.

"Find her!?" Kyle howled. "I'll kill her if I find her. She stole my dope." He grinned. "That's reason to kill her right there."

"There's never a good reason for killing people," Jan said, standing up. "It's not something anyone should ever *want* to do." With that, he made his way to the bathroom.

Kyle snickered. "Where'd you find this guy?"

"Belgium," I said. "I told you."

"I like him," he said. "But he's weird."

"No, he's not," I said, feeling as if it was my duty to defend Jan. "What's weird about him?"

But Kyle wasn't listening; his mind was elsewhere. "Is he rich?"

"I'm not sure," I said. "He deals gems."

"Gems?" Kyle screwed up his face. "Sounds rich." He gave me a light sock in the shoulder. "Why don't you knock him off and steal all his money?"

I didn't play along. Kyle's games went stale fast.

"He's not enough fun," Kyle said.

"What do you know about fun?"

Kyle smiled. "I'm here aren't I?"

I wished he wasn't. "Funny you should be."

Kyle gave me a blank look that was mildly disconcerting. I watched Jan making his way back to the table. A couple of women turned to look at him. He took his seat again. "Are we having one last round?"

"I am," Kyle said.

I shook my head. "I don't feel so well." I wanted to escape with Jan and leave Kyle to drink himself delirious.

Kyle said: "You never could drink." He slapped Jan on the back. "We'll get drunk together."

"Sure," Jan said. "I could have another." He sighed and raked his hand through his hair. "It was a long day."

"Tell me about it," Kyle said. "Every day of my fuckin' life is long."

I tried not to look too surprised. Kyle and Jan out for a night on the town? It was too bizarre.

I resolved not to leave Jan with Kyle. Carmi had plenty of booze for Jan to drink. I stood up. Jan didn't. It felt odd to tower over their heads for a change.

"I'll meet you later," he said, glancing at his watch. "Go ahead, especially if you don't feel well."

I felt stupid standing there with the two of them gawking at me. If they wanted to do the male-bonding thing, let them. Jan didn't seem like the chest-pounding type, but he didn't look unhappy either. I wasn't exactly pleased that he was staying, but I didn't want Jan to think I was a drag. So I said a cool good-bye and left. Outside, I realized it was still fairly early. Instead of hailing a cab, I wandered around for a while. The air was bracing. After a few blocks, I felt better. I ended up in a late-night bookstore and poked around the dusty shelves; the acrid odor of stale paper all around me. I wasn't in any hurry; I figured Kyle would keep Jan for at least an hour. I flipped though an old book about gems. It said that in India diamonds are supposed to protect you from danger.

chapter 16

When I got back to Carmi's, I jammed the right key into the wrong lock. I'd forgotten one of my uncle's prime directives: *Whatever you do,* he'd said, *don't put the top key in the bottom lock.* I yanked but the key wouldn't budge. Why Carmi never got the goddamn thing fixed was beyond me. I cursed up a storm. I'd have to wake the super; it was already after eleven.

As I started back to the elevator, I noticed Christian's door was slightly ajar. I thought about asking that pain in the ass to give me a hand. He'd love it—a damsel in distress. I waited in the hallway another minute trying to make up my mind. It dawned on me that he might not be alone. The lovely Giti was probably in there, getting a few lessons for her upcoming arranged marriage. I decided to risk embarrassing myself. I tapped on the door a few times, but no one answered. I knocked again, louder this time. I said, "Christian," as though I were taking attendance. Still nothing. Maybe he'd passed out and forgotten to slam the door closed behind him.

I gave it a push. The hinges squeaked. Inside, the lights were on. I called his name again. I stepped into the foyer and waited, listening for a sign of life. I imagined him sprawled on his bed, fancy shoes on the floor, wrinkled clothes half off. I smiled at the thought. "Christian," I repeated, tiptoeing across the room. I realized I'd never been in his place before. It was empty, save for a glass table with plastic Zip-loc bags spread across it and a black leather couch with a few magazines on the center cushion. I stepped on yesterday's paper; the pages rustled under my weight. The air was heavy with cigarette smoke. It was cold, too. I started to shiver. Somewhere, a window was open. I called his name again. The silence was unnerving.

In the bedroom, the lights were off. A strong wind sent the

curtains snapping and twisting like kites. I could make out the outline of Christian's sleeping body slumped against the far wall. Giti was nowhere to be seen. I edged closer to him, whispering his name over and over so as not to startle him. When I was at arm's length, I rested my palm on his bare shoulder. He'd passed out. He was as cool and smooth as a chilled apple. I shook him a little. "Christian," I said, waiting for him to jump up and scare me. "Christian," I said, slapping him hard. "Wake up." He was like a log. "Stop fooling around," I said, smacking him again. Still, he didn't move. I felt the first stroke of panic. I groped my way to the bureau and switched the lamp to its full vulgar brightness. It blinded me for a second.

Christian's hair was a thin veil over his face. His arms hung limply, his fingers curled into tight balls on the floor. I heard my breathing get louder. I repeated his name, but this time it was rhetorical. I stared at him, certain my mind was deceiving me. I couldn't move. I called out to him again, my voice no more than a croak. His downy curls were plastered to his head, thick with what had to be blood. I felt my sphincter tighten, my skin crawl. A rotting smell like bad tomatoes coated the inside of my nose and filled up my lungs. I leaned over the bureau and gagged up a taste so sour my eyes burned. In another glance, I saw the blood splat on the wall like a giant inkblot. I felt a knot of bile pushing its way into my throat. I puked all over the place. *Call the cops. Go to the phone and dial 911. Your neighbor's dead. Probably happened every night. The operators were used to it. Please come and scrape up my neighbor. He's beginning to stink up the place. We can't enjoy our dinner.*

A door slammed somewhere. But I couldn't take my eyes off Christian. I thought I heard my name. But I couldn't be sure. I was somewhere else now, where no one spoke English; I was privy to an espionage ring with guns and land mines and hit men. I was waiting for a subcommando with a goatee to adjudicate my fate. The next thing I knew, Jan was in front of me, his face a bunch of crevices. "What are you doing?" he whispered. I couldn't speak; my mouth was coated with something floury. Jan reached out and pressed two fingers against Christian's white neck. "He's dead," he said in his matter-of-fact way, his hands shaking. "Have you called the police?"

I shook my head. I was ready to wake up now.

Jan dragged me out of the apartment and into Carmi's. He pushed me onto the couch.

"Did you call?" he repeated.

"No," I said. I was crying now—nothing more than stunted hiccups.

Jan snatched the phone and dialed. I couldn't make out what he was saying. After he hung up, he opened the liquor cabinet and mixed me something strong. I downed it in one spasmodic gulp. Then I blacked out, like a severed wire, wondering how Jan managed to get the key out of the lock.

_____**PART II**

chapter 17

I don't remember much about the detective who questioned me (except that he stunk of garlic), or the police who combed the building, or the tenants who tried to sneak a peek at Christian's roped-off apartment. I was having a hard time sleeping. For the past three days, I'd had nightmares: I was standing over Christian's body when I felt hot breath on my neck. I woke up sweating, the sheets kicked to the foot of the bed. Jan kept me well supplied with over-the-counter sleeping pills—or maybe not; I didn't ask. I took whatever he gave me because they knocked me out. He also picked up groceries, kept the apartment clean, and generally felt sorry for me. I spoke to my parents a few times. They were ready to get on a plane and rescue me. But I convinced them I was fine. Besides, they'd spoil Carmi's vacation. He'd find out soon enough.

On the third day, I finally got up and made a decent breakfast. I felt my strength returning, the way you do after a week or two with the flu. I'd just finished my second cup of coffee when the doorman buzzed; Kyle was downstairs. I was surprised he'd condescended to the formality of buzzing. Maybe he knew about Christian, or maybe the doormen were becoming more vigilant. I guess a murder will do that. I let him up.

"You look like shit," he said by way of a greeting. He was right. This time, I was the one with the unwashed hair, white skin, and black circles under my eyes. Kyle didn't look any better.

"A lot's been going on," I said, as he gave me one of his rough hugs.

He wasn't listening. He was still checking me out. "You look like a druggie."

"It's temporary."

"That's my thing," Kyle said.

"Don't worry."

He laughed and made himself at home on the couch. "Where's Jan?"

"Working." He'd brought over Chinese last night. "I'm supposed to be at work, too," I said. "I called in sick."

Kyle giggled. "You're dissin' him."

I didn't bother to respond. I didn't have the energy. I rubbed my temples.

Kyle took a joint out of his pocket. "What's wrong with you?"

In Kyle's world, no one else could possibly have anything wrong. "My neighbor," I said, pointing at the wall. "He's dead."

"You're kidding," he said, scrunching up his freckled nose. "The Frenchy queer?"

I felt my eyes watering. "Swedish, at least he was."

Kyle stopped fidgeting with the joint. "Seriously?"

"Totally," I said. "He's dead. Someone bashed his head in."

He took a thoughtful drag. "Cool."

"I'm glad you find that titillating."

"I don't have a hard on, if that's what you mean."

You couldn't expect sympathy from Kyle. He wasn't capable of it. Regardless, there was something reassuring about his repellent predictability.

"You didn't like him anyway," he continued. "You said he was always tryin' to get some." He tapped ash into a mug. "I guess he won't be doing that anymore."

"I guess not." I hadn't told Kyle much about Christian except that we'd gone out a few times. Once in a while, I'd complained about Christian's unexpected drop-ins. As usual Kyle had drawn his own conclusions.

"What happened?"

"I found him in his bedroom." It sounded like I was making it up.

"What were you doing in his bedroom?"

"I came in late. His apartment door was open."

"Was he robbed?"

"No," I said.

"Not even his TV?" Kyle said.

"No."

"Then he was definitely into some very bad shit." He picked a bit of grass off his lip.

I rolled my eyes. "What makes you say that?"

Kyle exhaled and shook his head. "You didn't know anything about him."

"He was Swedish. He went to Columbia. He was an architect." I probably knew more about Christian than I did about Jan.

"Architect." Kyle snickered. "More like a mule."

"What are you talking about?"

"He was selling. Coke and weed and all kinds of good dope."

"I don't believe you." This was Kyle's way of getting me back.

"You should."

"Why should I?" My mind flashed to Christian's fat wad of hundreds. "What proof do you have?"

He twisted up his face. He was pissed off because I was sticking up for Christian. Kyle hated disloyalty. "I copped some blow from him a few times if you really want to know."

I almost jumped out of the chair. "What!"

He nodded coolly and smiled, pleased with the effect this was having. "That bastard sold me some of the best shit I ever had."

"You never told me," I said, sitting down.

"When he found out that I knew you," Kyle said. "He asked me not to."

"And you listened to him?"

"I was going to tell you . . . eventually."

I shook my head. Kyle's logic was ridiculous, convoluted. Beyond that, it was the stupidest thing I'd ever heard. I sat there staring at him; I wanted to reach over and belt him. It was so quiet I could hear the clock ticking from the bedroom. I got up, my head throbbing. I went into the kitchen and leaned over the sink. I peered into the narrow black drain, an image of Christian and Kyle crouched over a pile of balloons materialized out of nothing. "What's the big deal," Kyle said, following me into the kitchen and leaning on the counter next to me. "You jealous?"

"Why would I be jealous?" I almost screamed.

"Relax," Kyle said, scooting up to me. I could smell the tang of pot on his clothes.

"I am relaxed."

"He made me jealous," he said. "He got to hang out with you."

More stupidity. It was a miracle I didn't commit murder myself. "I hardly saw him."

"You saw him," he said, pressing his hands against my hip bones. "I watched you."

"Watched me?" I said, startled. I wondered if Kyle had been the one following me around. The idea gave me the creeps.

"Yeah." Kyle nodded, like it was an everyday thing for him. "I was keepin' an eye on you. . . ."

I felt a knot of crazy laughter working its way up my throat. "Who do you think you are?" I said, ready to throw him out. "My bodyguard?"

"I was just tryin' to help you out," he said, a pout clouding his face. "He said he was doin' you so I thought—"

"And you believed him?" I yelled.

"I was gonna tell you," Kyle said, leaning into me, the counter cutting me across the waist. "I really was."

With a guy like Kyle as your friend, you might as well not have any. I wondered how long he'd been "keeping an eye on me." It'd had been him all along. I wasn't crazy. I gave him a shove with my hip. "Get off me."

He took a step away. "Besides," he said, "he was a fag."

"Shut up," I said.

"He wanted to suck me off."

"Suck yourself off," I said, yelling again. "You're talking about someone who's dead."

But Kyle wouldn't give it up. "He wanted to kiss me first," he said. "So I told him forget it." He was smiling, his eyes were so puffy it was amazing he could see at all. "I swear."

"Get out."

Kyle put up his hands as though he was surrendering. Then he hulked back to the couch and lit another joint. I could hear the strike of the lighter. I stayed in the kitchen and waited for Kyle to vacate. I could barely look at him. Ten minutes later, still totally oblivious, he came back to the kitchen and asked me to go to a bar. Evidently, he was meeting a woman—a filmmaker who wanted him to be himself for her—which of course, turned him on. I wasn't interested and I sent him on his way.

Just as I was about to write Kyle off as the callow, no-good asshole he was, he called me from the street to say he was sorry about Christian; he was sorry he never told me about the dope; he was even sorrier that he'd said all that nasty shit—he actually liked Christian. For a Euro, he was all right. And for once in his life, Kyle actually sounded sincere.

chapter 18

About a week went by without any news from the cops. They were working Christian's case—collecting information, canvassing for witnesses, checking rap sheets. They didn't have much to go on. Christian's father came to claim his body. The cops didn't tell me anything else. Meanwhile, I kept having nightmares: Christian would make a nightly appearance, his hair matted with blood, his eyes black and blue. He wanted to know why I hadn't bothered to help him. I had a hard time defending myself. That's usually when I woke up—trapped by my inability to do anything. It was beginning to drive me crazy. It wasn't doing much for my professional life either: I called in sick for four more days. I figured Barneys would understand. Murder was a little worse than the flu.

Jan was a gentleman. He kept apologizing for not leaving the bar with me. If we had left together, then he would've discovered Christian, not me. He could've spared me the shock of stumbling upon a dead body. He seemed more upset by what I'd seen than by what had actually happened. He wasn't really depressed by the fact that Christian wasn't a part of this world anymore. I suppose you couldn't expect Jan to be devastated— he'd only met Christian twice. Jan tried to make me feel better with long walks and extravagant dinners. But I wasn't much company.

I wasn't much else either. We still hadn't slept together. It was the last thing on my mind. A murder can do that to you. Jan was the type of guy who could wait just about forever—unlike the hot-blooded Americans I'd known. In Belgium we'd had a lot of sex. But there was nothing else to do. He was on vacation and so was I. It'd happened naturally enough. For the time being, it seemed sacrilegious to have any fun so close to Christian's bad end.

The last time Jan attempted to entertain me, we'd gone to a

symphony at Carnegie Hall. I couldn't remember what we'd heard—something obscure and plaintive. I hadn't really wanted to go in the first place. I wore the shoes Christian had bought me. While he was alive, they'd sat in the box; I'd refused his pleas to wear them. Now I hardly took them off. They were excellent shoes—the best I'd ever owned. The leather had already molded to the shape of my feet, as though I'd had them for years. I liked the way they looked, too. Deceptively simple, but expensive. Sort of like Christian—you had to look twice.

During the three-hour concert, I'd nodded off—that's what Jan said—only to awake with a jerk. It was Christian again. This time the tables were turned. He was warning me: *Someone is after you.* I was laughing hysterically. Christian kept saying: *You are never taking me seriously.*

When the symphony finally concluded, Jan and I stopped in a nearby cafe. It was one of those clip joints with mediocre coffee and stale pastries. We sat facing one another in a booth, though my mind was still on Christian. If I thought about him enough, I'd figure out why he'd died. I could help him. In the middle of one of my many theories, Jan cut in. "You fell asleep during the symphony."

"I know," I said, slightly embarrassed.

"You were dreaming about him." Jan looked at me intently, his eyes two steady blue globes. I was caught offguard. Was he just guessing? Or had I said something in my sleep? I didn't ask. It was only normal that I'd be thinking about Christian. I said: "Christian, you mean?"

"Yes," he said. He seemed offended.

"I can't help it."

"You must've been close."

"Not really," I said, though I didn't mean it. Maybe I had been closer to Christian than I thought. It was only just becoming clear. I guess he'd been a friend. And now that he was gone, I missed him. I almost told Jan. But he was frowning.

"He was my next-door neighbor," I said.

"I know," he sighed, his mouth tightly drawn.

"I'm sorry," I said. "I know I haven't been much fun."

"It's not that," he said, but I could tell he was lying. "But you can't stop living when someone dies."

I hadn't. Jan expected me to have forgotten already. I told him so.

"I'm not sure the world will miss Christian as much as you do."

"What do you mean?"

"Maybe," Jan said, choosing his words carefully, "you're over-reacting a little."

"I don't think I am," I said. "I was the one who found him."

"I wish you hadn't."

"Well, I did," I said. "I can't change that."

"I know," Jan said. "I would change it if I could."

He sounded like he meant it. But there wasn't anything he could do.

"Did you know him so well?" Jan said. He laid out a twenty for the check and waved for our waitress.

"Not that well." I wasn't a good liar. I was sure he could probably tell. "We talked a few times."

Jan nodded. But he didn't prod any further. "Try not to think about it," he said. "We're together now." He smiled at me.

Maybe I was being selfish, spending what little time I had with Jan thinking about Christian. Jan drained his espresso, stubbed out his cigarette, and slid off the banquet. "In time," he added, "you'll forget."

chapter 19

It was a relief to get back to the dumb-dumb world of retail. As soon as I showed up, Malcolm assaulted me with questions. He demanded to know everything, every gruesome detail. I'd already gone over the whole story on the phone with him. I was beginning to bore myself. But Malcolm wouldn't be deterred. He said, "Tell me again and start from the beginning."

"I already told you," I said. "I came home from the bar . . ."

Malcolm nodded and mumbled, "I know, I know," as if I was beginning in the wrong place.

"I'd been there with Jan and Kyle. I left about ten thirty and went to the used bookstore. You know the one on the corner—"

"Yes, yes," he said, cutting me off. "Get to the good stuff."

"I poked around for a while. Then I took a cab home. It must've been around midnight. I got the wrong key in the lock. My uncle warned me. He'd said—"

"I know, I know," Malcolm said, shaking a pair of eyelet ankle socks at me. "Get to the most sordid of details, the dead body!"

"I'm getting there," I said. "Will you hold on?"

"It's just so Hitchcock, so early DePalma. I can't stand it. I wish it'd been me. I really do. To find a *body*, how utterly . . . utterly . . ." His voice trailed off. He scribbled a note on the back of a receipt.

"So," I said. "I saw Christian's door open. I went in. I kept saying his name, but he didn't answer. The whole place stunk like bad tomatoes. I went into the bedroom and there he was . . . slumped against the wall." Malcolm sucked in his breath. "I thought he'd passed out. But the smell. I turned on the lamp and saw his hair. It was matted with blood. Like fruit pulp. Then I sort of blanked out. The next thing I knew I was back in my apartment; Jan had brought me there. I guess I must've passed out.

That's it. That's what happened." I was sweating. Just talking about it sent me back—my own private horror flick.

"What about suspects? What about motives? What about a weapon?" Malcolm was disappointed. It wasn't *Law & Order* enough for him. He kept going. "Who did it? How'd the killer get into the building? Isn't there a doorman? What did *he* say? What did the police say? Are *you* a suspect?"

"Of course I'm not a suspect!"

"Don't get all riled up," he said, taking a turn around the sock display. "I'm just trying to get the facts."

"Maybe you ought to become a detective."

He made a face. "I'm a television artiste specializing in human brutality."

"Oh, yeah. I forgot." He was still at Barneys because human brutality didn't yet pay the rent.

"You know," Malcolm said, smiling conspiratorially, "maybe it was an accidental thing. Something from the auto-erotic, it-feels-so-good-to-hurt-yourself school of pleasure?"

"I don't think so. The police would've told me that."

"Don't bet on it." Malcolm rubbed the stubble on his chin. He was engrossed in his latest theory. "I have to tell you," he said. "I thought he was kinky."

"Kinky?"

"He was just so perfectly formed. Angelic in every way. Those are the kind to watch out for." He sniffled and wagged a finger at me.

I shook my head. "I never saw any whips or chains." Our lone fuck was as conventional as it got. Even the Catholic Church would've approved.

"There's something else I heard," I said, as a pod of Japanese tourists clopped across the floor. "Not that I believe it."

"What?"

"Supposedly he was . . . dealing."

"You mean drugs, of course."

"No," I said. "Vacuum cleaners."

"Funny," Malcolm said, frowning. "You did say he liked to shop, especially at this dump. And to indulge, baby, you have to have a bulge . . ."

"He always had a lot of cash on him," I said. "I should've guessed . . ."

"Don't blame yourself," Malcolm said, pursing his lips. "I've known dealers who'd trade car coats for kilos." He winked like I should know what he was talking about.

I took a hard look at Malcolm. Was he referring to his own backdoor deals? I'd heard rumors around Barneys about certain expensive items suddenly going missing; a girl he'd worked with in jewelry said they'd gone up his nose. But these were rumors. Malcolm didn't strike me as having a five-hundred-a-week habit. Though I'd been wrong before—very wrong. And he always seemed to have a cold. . . .

Malcolm didn't give me long to consider my latest idea. He spent the morning chattering about Christian's tragic end. Christian having some fun with a door hook and belt; Christian the pusher and his network of high-rent clients; Christian the Corybant hosting orgies with dildos and horse whips. At the end of the day, I still thought it was all bullshit. Christian had been murdered, randomly. It could've been anybody. It could have been me.

Then, as I was wrapping a cashmere cardigan in tissue, Malcolm recounted one last tidbit that bugged me. Supposedly, a "red-haired wild-eyed giant" had stormed through Barneys demanding to know where I was. He'd even asked baffled customers. The giant in question was unmistakably Kyle. According to Malcolm, Kyle had said vile, glass-chewing things to him, mainly because he'd refused to reveal my whereabouts. Kyle had also accused Malcolm of being a pseudo-Genet. "Can you imagine?" Malcolm said. "That cretin had the audacity to insult my art." I suddenly thought about Malcolm's play. I'd never returned it and I was surprised Malcolm hadn't asked me for it back. I couldn't recollect when or where I'd last seen his manuscript. It bothered me slightly. Had I thrown it out with a pile of old newspapers by mistake? And it was bizarre that Kyle knew of Malcolm's work, though he'd recently been building sets for Off-Off Broadway theater. Why hadn't Kyle told me about his visit to Barneys? Maybe he'd forgotten. Regardless, he'd made a bad impression on Malcolm. Malcolm, a student of the Carmi School of Neurosis, said I should be more cautious—perhaps Kyle had slain Christian in a jealous rage. "Maybe," he said, "your friend is a murderer!" It was so unlikely it was funny. Kyle, the big lumbering coward, a killer. Still, Kyle had taken up a new habit—following me around—that didn't make me feel very comfortable.

Near the end of the day, I got a call from Barneys' Human Resources Department. They wanted to see me right away. They said it had nothing to do with my calling in sick. They truly understood. Something like this had happened to another one of their employees; someone had died in his bed. But it was simply a matter of downsizing. Things were slow and I was the last person to be hired—low man on the totem pole, so to speak. And would I mind so much being escorted out of the building? Would I mind relinquishing my swipe card? I could pick up my last check next week. As I marched through the CO/OP with a security guard lightly holding my elbow, Malcolm shrieked: "Fascist pickle-eating bastards!" I laughed. It wasn't very painful leaving. My time was almost up there—Carmi'd be back in two weeks. I suppose, in some way, it marked the beginning of the end.

chapter 20

When Jan found out that I'd been canned, he canceled his appointments and met me outside the Metropolitan Museum of Art. It was the first time I'd seen him in a suit. He wore gray flannel well, and I told him so. He said I looked better than I had since all of this began. Then he kissed me for a while, his cheeks rough against my skin. He seemed lighter, his step jauntier—maybe it was just me. I was feeling better than I had since Christian died. I was almost myself again. And I was ready to be with Jan.

He wanted to look at the nineteenth-century paintings. We wandered from gallery to gallery. Jan skimmed the placards. I thought about all the times I'd gone to museums with Kyle. He'd run helter-skelter around the galleries like a kid in a toy store, shouting my name from halfway across a room while other museumgoers stared. Kyle delighted in what he liked; he dismissed anything that even slightly bored him. Jan was thorough and knowledgeable. I was somewhere in between.

Today I kept pace with Jan. We held hands off and on and talked about nothing in particular. Eventually, we wound up on a smooth wooden bench in front of one of Gauguin's Tahitian paintings. Jan was very close to me; the scent of his faded cologne wafted around us.

"Did you know Gauguin was a brokerage clerk?" he said.

I shook my head.

"He started painting when he was twenty-six."

"Amazing," I said, feeling very unaccomplished.

"So there's hope." He turned toward me and smiled. "For me."

"Do you want to paint?"

"I can barely draw," he said, laughing. "I just like the idea that you can start late."

"I know what you mean," I said. I was on my way to being a late bloomer.

Jan nodded, then his smile faded. "You know I'm only here for a short time," he said.

From his letter, I knew that Jan hadn't expected to stay long. Still, I didn't want to think about his leaving.

"I know," I said. "I'll miss you when you're gone."

"I have an idea."

"What?"

"Why don't you come with me?" he said, slipping his arm around my shoulders. "Just for a few days. To get away from all this . . ."

I couldn't—that was my first response. I couldn't be so irresponsible. It wasn't in my genes. But Jan was prepared. He'd already thought his plan through. "You could," he said, "if you wanted to."

Jan was right. I could do whatever I wanted. At the moment, my plan was to go back to California and figure out what to do with my life. My parents, mortified by what had happened in New York, had my room all ready and a bunch of help-wanted ads already circled on my desk. For now, I had no obligations. I was free. California could always wait. Of course, there was the problem of money. I had my meager savings from the Barneys gig. It was enough for a security deposit on a cramped apartment in San Francisco. Jan seemed to read my mind.

"I'll take care of everything," he said, nodding as though his mind was already running through a list. "You don't have to worry."

"Where would we go?" I said, pretending we were on our way.

Jan shrugged. "Wherever. As long as we're together. It doesn't matter."

With that, he got up and inspected the Gauguin. "Tahiti might be nice. I've never been." He looked back at me as if to say, *Well, are you game?*

I took in his determined face and for the first time it occurred to me that I could go. Maybe it would do me good. I recalled how happy Jan and I had been in Belgium. Tahiti or anywhere tropical was better than Europe in the winter. But what would I do when I returned from fantasy island?

In the cab back to Carmi's, Jan held my hand tightly and looked out the window. I was still thinking about his proposal—if you could call it that—as Fifth Avenue flew by outside. It was late afternoon and the midtown skyscrapers were beginning to take on a soft saffron color. People spilled onto the sidewalks rushing to get ahead. I wondered where they were all going.

"I've been thinking a lot," Jan said, still gazing out the window.

"About what?" I said.

"Christian."

I hadn't expected Jan to be thinking about Christian.

"I'm sorry about what happened," he said.

I asked him what he meant.

"I think I could've been more . . . sympathetic," Jan said, turning toward me. His face was ruddy. He looked upset.

"It's okay," I said. "It's been hard all around." We drove on past the Empire State Building. He put his arm around me. I closed my eyes and enjoyed it.

Back at Carmi's, Jan wanted to listen to a jazz station. It was the same way in Belgium—a strange prelude to making love. He had his eyes closed like he was meditating; a tenor sax surged from the speakers. Through the window I could see flurries beginning, wild minuets of snow circling until they hit something solid and melted away.

the foreigner_____**MEG CASTALDO**

Finally, Jan kissed me on the mouth for a long time, as though he was savoring a morsel. I remembered he had a slow way of kissing—he had all the time in the world; he could go on kissing for days, even years. He tasted delicious, like sugary coffee. When he pulled away, he said: "We've remembered each other again?"

"I don't think I ever forgot you."

He kissed me while his hands crawled across my shirt. One by one he undid the buttons. It was almost excruciating. Somehow I managed to slip out of my jeans. The more I squirmed around, the slower he became, creeping along at reptilian speed. After a while he stood up and stripped, draping his clothes over a chair. He rubbed his flat stomach. I stayed on the couch, taking in his body again. He was as white as a potato, save for a few dark moles. I remembered now that they were dry as sandpaper and I'd tried not to touch them. His feet were bony and crowlike. I'd forgotten about them, too. It all came back to me; we could've been in the inn with the blue shutters again. With Jan, making love was constant, the same note over and over. It was like a Sufi ritual. Or a marathon.

"I've missed you," he said, lying down on me, the odor of talc on his skin.

I mumbled the same.

He slid his arms under me, resting his spidery hands on my bra. He stood up again and wiggled out of his underwear. He was big and crooked, a long flap covered the tip like a piece of soft folded leather. I wrapped my hand around it. He shuddered then pushed against my lips. I let him into my mouth. A drop of salty liquid passed over my tongue. Eventually, he pulled away from me, peeled off my panties, and climbed on top of me. He had his hands near my ears, his chest above my face. He slid in and lazily began pumping. I closed my eyes. I was sweating, trying to get comfortable, trying to find the right rhythm. The radiator clanged in the background, a musky odor filled the room. I pushed my heels into his flat butt, squirming underneath him. Jan was breathing hard, his face buried in the pillow above my head. I clutched his back, spreading my legs as wide as I could. I'd forgotten the somber quality of our sex. Jan didn't make any noise, not even a grunt—a stark contrast to the screamers I'd been with. I was unusually quiet, too. I was afraid to make any noise. It seemed forbidden. We came all at once in silence and Jan collapsed on me like a pile of bricks. When he caught his breath, he rolled off and picked up his cigarettes. He fidgeted with the box, the lighter, shaking it up and down. Then he said: "Alex, I have to ask you something."

I rolled over on my elbow. "What?" I said.

"Have you been with someone else?"

I didn't answer him. It must've been obvious.

"Of course," Jan said. "We didn't have any agreements."

There wasn't anything to say. A few moments passed. Then I had to ask: "Have you?"

"What?"

"Been with someone?" Not that I really wanted to know.

He let out a long sigh that I took for a yes. The room began to gray. "Forget it," Jan said. "It means nothing." I wasn't sure I agreed with him. There was something about the way Jan looked at me that made me wonder if he knew I'd been with Christian. I felt guiltier now than when I'd actually slept with my neighbor like a bored housewife. The feeling nagged me for the rest of the night.

chapter 21

Later that evening, when I got back from dinner with Jan, I found about ten frantic messages from Kyle. In fact, he'd covered the whole tape with a single repeated request: Would I please meet him at a pastry shop called DiRobertis in the East Village—he needed to tell me something. It was on such and such street. I could take such and such train. I wouldn't get lost. He'd even walk me home if I met him. I couldn't imagine what he wanted. And the idea appealed to me less than it would've in the past. Lately, I wasn't sure what Kyle was actually up to. I had the distinct feeling that something was going on behind my back . . . a plot being hatched like some political maneuver in the Politburo. Still, I gave in, if only because my paranoia was usurped by a silly sense of loyalty. That, and Kyle's tone. It was so un-Kyle I was actually concerned.

When I finally got to DiRobertis, Kyle, of course, was nowhere to be seen. I cursed him. Then I cursed myself for giving in to his hysteria. I'd wait a half hour—no more. My hands and feet were so cold it'd take that long to thaw. I needed coffee.

I slid into a vinyl booth facing the door. I couldn't see much. The entrance was obscured by glass vitrines piled high with pastries. DiRobertis had been around since 1898—it looked it. The mosaic floor was missing a tile here and there, though it was still pretty. Faded black-and-white photos of the Old Country dotted the walls—the faces reminded me of my own family. The place smelled heavenly, like fresh coffee and molten sugar. I ordered a pignoli cake and a cappuccino from a hunched waiter who must've been here since opening day. Then I waited.

I was about to leave when Kyle tumbled through the door, his eyes wild. He made a beeline for me and sprawled into the booth like it was a relief to get off his feet.

"You're late," I said, draining my cappuccino.

"I know," he said, yanking off his watchman's cap. "I got held up. I'm really sorry."

That was a surprise. A second apology from Kyle. He never apologized. Either way, I was still annoyed. I wanted to know what pressing piece of business required dragging me here. "Well?" I said.

Kyle fumbled with his cigarettes. Then he flagged the little waiter and ordered coffee and two cannolis. "I need a sugar rush," he said.

"I asked you a question," I said, sounding like a parent trying to tear the truth out of a child. He still hadn't answered me.

"I know," he said. "Can you wait a friggin' minute?" He shook his head. "I'm gettin' to it."

I tried to figure out what was on Kyle's mind, but he was stone-faced. He was twitchy, too, which wasn't anything new for Kyle. He kept craning his neck toward the door, as if he half-expected to see someone he knew.

"Can I sit over there?" he said.

"Why?"

"Because," he grumbled. "I want to see the door."

I shrugged and changed seats with him. "Better?" I said.

"Yeah," he said. "Whatever."

Kyle usually had a sense of humor; without it he wasn't much fun. The waiter crept to the table and dumped off his order. He wolfed down the cannolis and slurped his coffee. I was still waiting to hear what he had to tell me, his great revelation. Kyle pushed back his plate and wiped his mouth with the back of his hand. I noticed his fingers were all black and blue.

"Jesus," I said. "What happened to your hands?"

He looked down at them as though he didn't remember himself. Then he said: "I got them slammed in between a pile of sheet rock. This fuckin' Czech guy wasn't payin' attention." Apparently, he'd spent the day building a set for an improv company in Brooklyn.

"It looks sore," I said.

He made a face. "It is."

We sat there for a few more minutes, Kyle looking over his shoulder every so often. "I asked you to come here," he said in a low voice, "because I wanted to see you."

"That's it?"

He looked hurt. "I wanted to see if you're okay."

It was nice to know Kyle cared so much. But it was also unlikely.

"And?"

He nodded. "You seem okay."

I thought he was alluding to Christian. "I'm still upset," I said, "If that's what you mean."

"Yeah," he said. "I guess that's what I mean."

"It keeps coming back to me."

"It would," he said.

"It'll take a while."

The waiter refilled our coffee. Kyle took a sip and burned his tongue. "Fuck," he said.

I laughed. I couldn't help myself. I wondered why Kyle was so concerned about me. He hadn't been a week ago. Maybe it was delayed guilt. But Kyle didn't feel guilty the way other people did. It didn't make any sense. Before I could pry into his complicated head, he said: "How did Christian get whacked?"

It was a pretty standard question coming from Kyle. He'd always been fascinated by blood and guts and gore. Christian's mushy skull came back to me as clearly as a photograph. "His head got smashed into a wall."

Kyle nodded then looked around. We were the only customers in the place. "What's wrong with you?" I said. He was beginning to make me nervous. And I'd been nervous enough these last few days.

"Nothin'," he said. "It's the fuckin' coffee. It's making my ears ring."

I slid the cup away from him.

"Hey," he said.

"Enough," I said.

"So he got his head smashed in?"

I nodded.

"Anything else?"

"Like what?"

He shrugged. "I don't know."

I wondered what he was getting at now. "Then why ask?"

"People get dead in this town all the time."

"Obviously," I said.

But Kyle wasn't listening. He was pulling his cap down over his ears like he was trying to disappear. "I'm just tryin' to understand," he said.

"Understand what?"

"This Christian shit," he said, his eyes pinned on mine.

"What are you saying?" I said. Cold perspiration began to collect under my arms.

He shook his head. "It's all fucked up. I don't even know who's being straight and who's not. All I know," he said, throwing a ten on the table, "is that someone is pretty pissed off about the way things got left by your Euro."

"What things?" I wanted him to come right out and say it.

"I can't say 'cause I don't know."

Kyle liked to think he knew everything. This was a surprise. "Are you for real?"

"I've been hearin' shit," Kyle said. "That's all."

"From who?"

Kyle shook his head. "You don't want to know."

"It's not a matter of wanting."

Kyle kept shaking his head.

"This drug thing?" I said.

"Just be a little careful. That's all."

"Careful." I said the word like I didn't know the meaning. "What genius are you hearing this shit from?"

"I already told you," Kyle said. "You don't want to know."

I frowned. This was too much.

"Trust me."

That was the whole problem. I didn't trust Kyle.

"I'm trying," I said.

"Tryin' to what?"

"Trust you."

Kyle sat up straight. "You don't trust me?"

"You never even told me about Christian," I said.

"You're bringing that up again?"

I didn't say anything.

Kyle groaned. "I was gonna tell you. I only traded a few lousy bucks for a couple of lines of coke." He put up his hands. His fingers reminded me of black licorice whips. "That's all."

"I believe you," I said, "if that makes you feel any better."

"Gee, thanks." He smiled sourly.

A few minutes passed. The waiter brought the check. Kyle dropped a pile of coins onto the table. Then he said he had to split. He'd call me later. With that, he was gone. I decided to stay and think about what Kyle had said over a second cappuccino. The bottom line was Christian had pissed someone off. But

Kyle's imagination had a tendency to take on a literary quality—literary and delusional. It was one of the reasons I'd always stuck with him. And who knew what weird substance was petering out in his veins now. The whole sordid thing made me long for California. I'd be glad to get out of New York. It was the sort of place where you could get run over by a bus.

chapter 22

When I left the pastry shop, it was freezing. I hurried back to Carmi's. The temperature seemed to be dropping by the second. My ears and toes ached. I quickened my pace. I had the sense that someone was on my heels—again. I was making myself crazy. I looked over my shoulder expecting to see Kyle. But there wasn't anyone who looked suspicious—or familiar. Just the usual anonymous faces buried under scarves and hoods. I crossed to the other side of the street. I couldn't help myself. If I didn't get out of New York soon, I'd have to see a shrink. I was imagining myself lying on a black Herman Miller chaise, blabbing about a dream, when I felt a hand on my arm. I spun to my left thinking it'd be Kyle. But it was Yassi. Her face was wind-burned like she'd spent the entire day outside. I was furious. I tried to shake her off, but she yanked me so hard I nearly lost my balance. A man in a shabby coat passed by. I tried to catch his eye. He paused but didn't stop. Somehow Yassi managed to drag me into a shadowy alley that reeked of urine. She had her hand wrapped around my upper arm. She was a lot stronger than I would've guessed.

"We've got to talk," she said, finally.

She relaxed her grip but didn't let go.

"Get off me," I hissed.

But Yassi wasn't paying attention. She glanced around wildly. The alley was long, dank, and dimly lit. I could reach out and touch the moldy brick buildings on either side. Yassi unzipped her thick camouflage parka and showed me what looked like a toy pistol—I'd never seen a real one—strapped to her pale fleshy belly. "Shut your mouth, okay?"

Something inside me told me to laugh. It wasn't by any

means natural. A choked off, frightened twitter. Yassi wasn't amused. She still had my arm, the pistol visible beneath her jacket. I felt faint . . . I hoped I wouldn't pass out.

She gave me a careful look. "Don't do anything dumb," she said. Then she let go of me.

"What do you *want?*" I asked. My voice was hoarse, though it hadn't been five minutes ago.

"It's about Christian," she said, rubbing her peach-fuzz scalp. "What else?"

I couldn't believe it: first Kyle, now Yassi. Did Christian associate with every goddamn person I knew in New York? "You're joking?" I whispered.

"Why would I make jokes?" she said, narrowing her bloodshot gray eyes.

"I don't know," I said. "But this isn't funny."

"Am I laughing?"

I shook my head. What had Christian gotten himself into . . . what had he gotten *me* into? I tried to get a read on Yassi. But she wasn't exactly playing with a full deck. I hoped she wouldn't do anything irrational. It occurred to me that I should bolt out of the alley, run away, scream—do something. But the sight of that gun—was it even real?—kept me rooted to the pavement, sweating. Would she shoot me in public?

"My sister . . . ," she interrupted, chewing on a ragged index finger, "was Christian's girlfriend."

"Your sister?" I repeated. I was too dumbfounded to say anything else.

Yassi nodded. "Giti. Her name is Giti."

I recalled the woman I'd seen with Christian in the lobby of Carmi's building. She had to have been . . . Giti. *That's* why Yassi had seemed so familiar. They did look similar. Yassi was paler, more bedraggled, but they had the same alien gray eyes.

"I need your help," she said, stepping closer to me. Her combat boots crushing broken glass. "I like you . . ."

I opened my mouth then closed it. Yassi had a weird way of showing affection. I didn't want to get on her bad side. "What do you want from me?" I managed to croak.

"I want you to keep your mouth shut," she said, "for starters."

My mouth shut. What was she talking about? I nodded. Given the circumstances, it was better to agree.

"You're all right," she cackled. "For a bourgeoisie."

I might've laughed if I hadn't thought she'd shoot me. I took a few paces back. Maybe I'd just start running . . . you could survive a gunshot to the back, couldn't you?

"I want to talk about Kyle," Yassi said.

"Kyle?" I said. "What about Christian?"

"Forget Christian," she said. "He's dead . . . he was stupid." She lit a cigarette and handed it to me. I smoked, even though I didn't want to. It seemed like a bad idea to say no.

"What do you mean stupid?"

"He just was," she said. "He acted like a sucking movie star." She shook her head. "Never mind. That's not why we're here."

Kyle had told me that Yassi had a tendency to flip out over the tiniest affronts. Anecdotes were coming back to me now. Things he'd said that I'd dismissed as tall tales . . . she'd smacked a construction worker across the face for whistling at her . . . nonsense about the Algerian revolution . . . she did have a gun, I reminded myself. I wished she'd get to the point.

"I want you to warn Kyle . . . ," she commanded, exhaling a lung's worth of smoke. "About what's coming."

The hairs on the back of my neck stood up. Kyle had alluded

to something terrible. Why couldn't she warn him? I almost suggested it.

"I'd do it myself," Yassi said, "but I can't. We don't talk."

I'd forgotten—they'd "broken up."

I couldn't either. Whatever Kyle had fallen into was serious. I wanted no part of it.

"He'll call you," she said, bluntly. "He always does." She threw down her butt and smashed it with her steel-enforced toe.

"Don't be so sure . . ." I ventured. Kyle had a tendency to go missing for days, even weeks.

"He will," she said, steadying her gaze, like she'd finally adjusted the lens on a camera.

"Alex," she commanded, again. "You're getting it, right."

"I'm getting it," I repeated, confidently, even though I wasn't. What was there to get?

She slowly zipped up her jacket. Was the interrogation over?

"One more thing . . . ," she said, sauntering toward the street. "Don't even think about going to the cops."

I had thought about it. But I put up my hands as though I was surrendering. "Don't worry."

A wry smile came over her pinched face. It didn't soften her in the slightest. "I know where you live . . ."

I stood there like a fool, nodding as though someone had just finished giving their opinion on a Senate race.

Yassi was halfway to the sidewalk by now. I was almost free. Abruptly, she stopped, turned on her heel, and stormed toward me. I held my breath. Here it comes, I thought . . . I closed my eyes. When I opened them, she was right in my face, her voice low and deliberate. "Listen, *Alex*. Kyle fucked with the network . . . and some bad shit is coming. That's all I'm saying." She pulled a black beret over her eyes. "I'm outta here," she said. "I'm leaving the country. Tomorrow. Tell Kyle not to look for me—anywhere. That goes for the whole sucking planet. Tell him not to waste his time." In a moment, she was gone. I was left at the mouth of the alley, shivering.

Back at Carmi's, I forced down a tall gin and tonic. I hoped it would quell my anxiety. The only thing I got was a sour stomach. Yassi's face kept materializing, her tinny voice ringing in my ears. Christian crossed my mind, too—*You are liking the fun, no?* Then, of course, there was Kyle. If he had a phone, I would've called and thanked him for practically getting me killed. In the meantime, I was intent on figuring out how compromised I was.

I went over the scene in the pastry shop with Kyle. Why had he been so paranoid? Was he worried that Yassi was going to come after him? And what the hell for? What about his hands? Had he really gotten them smashed by sheet rock? If Kyle thought he was in trouble, he'd certainly tell me—or would he? Maybe he'd been hooked into a deal that went south. With Kyle that was always a possibility. Maybe by association, I was guilty, too. And what the hell was the "network"?

I didn't know what to make of Yassi; she didn't strike me as a killer . . . but she *did* carry a gun. I guess I only half-believed the stuff she said. For now, I'd do nothing. If I heard from Kyle, I'd relay her cryptic message. As for the cops, I wouldn't call. Not yet. But if something else happened . . .

Around seven the next morning the phone rang. I almost jumped out of my skin. I thought it'd be Kyle. I was wrong.

"Hello . . . Alex?"

I heard a beep—the international operator. "Yes?"

"It's Uncle Carmi." I'd almost forgotten about him.

"Hi, Carmi," I said, with as much cheer as I could muster.

"How are you, dear?"

"Fine." I'd save the good news for later.

"That's nice." I heard Spanish in the background—a man's voice. Carmi shot something off to him.

There was a pause. "So how are you?" I said.

"Fine," Carmi said. "Best I've ever been."

"Having fun?"

He chuckled. "Lots."

"Great."

"Staying out of trouble?" he said.

"Of course."

"You know, Alex. It's been a relief knowing you're there." There was another pause. "I haven't worried about a thing." The line cracked and popped. "The phones are very bad here."

"All right, then, Carmi. I won't keep you."

"You're not keeping me, Alex." Carmi let out a small cough. "I wonder, dear, have you seen my neighbor, Christian Olsen?"

I swallowed a knot that had collected in my throat. "Not recently." That was true.

"He didn't drop anything off for me?"

"No, Carmi," I said. Especially not now. "Nothing."

"That's odd," he sighed. "Oh, well."

"We're you expecting something?" I recalled the message he'd left me. I couldn't imagine what Christian could've possibly had for Carmi.

"It's a long story, Alex."

"What do you—" A piercing noise came over the phone. We lost contact for a second or two. "Carmi?" I said. "Carmi?"

"Okay, dear," he said. "I'm losing you."

"What was Christian supposed to give you?" I said.

"I can't hear you," he said. "I'll call you again."

the foreigner_____**MEG CASTALDO**

"Wait," I said.

"Bye-bye."

"Bye, Carmi." I said, but he was already gone.

I hung up. What in the hell was Carmi expecting from Christian?

chapter 23

I hadn't seen Jan for two days. He'd been stuck at a gem convention in New Jersey; he was so apologetic I was hardly offended. He suggested we meet at a midtown hotel. He had to drop off something for a client. Then we'd have dinner, if that was okay with me. Yassi was still fresh in my mind. I was edgy, though my anxiety was slowly fading. I wasn't going to wait around for Kyle to call. How would Yassi know if I warned him or not? And was she really threatening me? Should I take her seriously? Getting out of the apartment seemed like a good idea; sitting around worrying wasn't making me feel any better. I'd have the doorman hail me a cab. I'd get dropped off in front of the hotel. What could possibly happen?

When I arrived, I spotted Jan and a guy I assumed was his client—a dark man with close-cropped hair clad in a navy suit. They were perched on a white settee engrossed in conversation. As I crossed the lobby, I watched them. They seemed familiar, as though they'd known each other for years. When I was practically standing in front of him, Jan got up and kissed me lightly. Then he dragged a chair over and introduced me to Eddie Nazir.

"It is a pleasure," Eddie said.

"Likewise," I said. Eddie was about thirty-five, slight, and brown with soft black eyes.

After a moment, Jan excused himself to refill our drinks. I wished he hadn't. I wasn't in a talkative frame of mind.

"I am very sorry," Eddie said. "About your friend."

"Thank you," I said, not knowing what else to say. I couldn't fathom why Jan had told him about Christian. Though the way things were going, it might as well be on the evening news.

"You must feel terribly sad," he said.

"It's pretty awful," I said. Thinking about Christian made me feel depressed all over again.

"A tragedy," he said, staring into his empty glass.

"Shakespearean," I said.

"Things like this happen all the time in my country."

"What's your country?"

"Pakistan."

I didn't feel any better knowing people got killed in Pakistan.

"He was very much a perfectionist," Eddie said.

"Who?" I said.

"Christian, of course." Eddie looked embarrassed.

I leaned back in my chair to brace myself. "You knew him?"

"Ah, yes," Eddie said, showing off a dazzling smile. "It is a small world, no?"

I couldn't imagine any world this small. It seemed like Christian knew the entire planet. I must've looked pretty shell-shocked because Eddie said: "I sold to him."

I had to keep myself from blurting out: *Drugs?*

"He was very, very critical," Eddie continued. "My rugs were never quite right."

Rugs, not drugs. That, at least, made sense. "For his . . . architectural projects?"

"Yes."

"You sell carpets?"

"Kilims."

"Oh."

"I export," he said. "Kilims, fabrics, wrought-iron figurines. Christian was very discerning. He had a client with a compli-cated kitchen."

I was about to ask him about the complicated kitchen when Jan returned with our drinks. A gin and tonic for me; scotch for Jan and Eddie. They fell back into the easy conversation of old friends. Eddie had just bought a fire opal for his sister. They chatted about London while I brooded over my latest discovery. Could it all just be a coincidence? Maybe this was the guy who'd called Christian on his cell phone. I waited for the opportunity to ask. But Eddie announced that he had a dinner engagement—would we mind excusing him? He squeezed my hand, thanked Jan, and left.

I drained my gin and tonic; a shard of lime pulp lodged itself between my teeth. "Where does he export?"

"All over," Jan said.

"Here, too?"

"Americans love rugs," Jan said, smiling. "Why do you care?"

"He knew Christian," I said.

"I know."

"He told you?"

"Yes," Jan said, striking a match and lighting a cigarette. "Eddie said he knew him. But not well."

"Don't you think that's weird?"

"Not weird," Jan said, taking a thoughtful puff. "Just a coincidence."

That sounded familiar. The gin had gone—as usual—to my head. I thought about telling Jan about Kyle and Yassi. But I was afraid he'd march me straight to the police and make me tell them everything. I wasn't sure I believed their nonsense. But this Eddie person was another matter.

"This can't all be a coincidence," I said.

"What do you mean?"

"I mean: Why is this guy Eddie your client? And how did he know Christian? Don't you think that's odd?" I tried to keep my voice even.

"I already told you," Jan said emphatically. "It is odd."

I didn't know what I expected from Jan. He agreed with me.

the foreigner_____**MEG CASTALDO**

He thought it was a coincidence—period. I was reading into things too deeply. Still, I couldn't help feeling that a giant plot had begun to shrinkwrap around me. There was only one thing to do: I sent Jan for another drink.

By the time we descended the bamboo steps to the quiet Japanese restaurant that Jan had picked out, I was feeling okay. I'd convinced myself I didn't care about Eddie and his rugs or Yassi and her threats or Kyle and his ringing ears. I was far away from all that now, tucked underground with twinkling Kyoto music burbling overhead. A woman in a kimono and obi greeted us. Jan tried to interest me in shabu-shabu, but my appetite didn't seem to be functioning. He resorted to analyzing the menu. After he ordered and the waitress left, Jan took my hand and said: "I'm worried about you."

"I'm fine."

"You're . . . obsessing," he said.

"I'm not obsessing."

I must've seemed hurt because he said: "Maybe that's not the right word."

"Then what is?"

He sighed. "I don't know," he said, shaking his head. "Preoccupied, maybe."

"I can't help it."

"I know."

I shook my head. I wanted to tell Jan the entire story. But all of this was partly my fault for fooling around with Christian in the first place. I didn't want to involve Jan. Yassi said I should keep my mouth shut. Her warning lingered like the burned taste on my tongue from the cigarette I hadn't wanted. I decided that if something else went wrong, I'd tell Jan.

The waitress dumped a gondola-size tray of sushi between

us. Jan unfurled his chopsticks and poured soy sauce into two tiny dishes. Then he looked up at me with his steady blue eyes. "Try to eat," he said, pushing the tray toward me. "You're beginning to look like Twiggy."

At least Jan had kept his sense of humor. I pulled apart my chopsticks—one splintered. I wasn't unusually superstitious, but it seemed like a bad omen, as though I'd never be able to make a clean break from Christian and his mysterious demise. I took two pieces of shrimp. I'd never been a huge fan of raw fish; the texture reminded me of Jell-O.

As we ate, Jan talked about the convention, the people he'd met and the things he'd bought. I knew he was hoping to get my mind off Christian. I liked him even more for it. Still, my mind drifted back to Eddie. I tried not to let on that I wasn't all there. I was in two places at once. Listening and commenting on what Jan was saying. And racing through my conversation with Eddie Nazir, rug exporter. I wished I'd had a chance to ask Eddie if he'd called Christian on his cell phone. The strange language Christian had spoken in Carmi's apartment came back to me. Would a Pakistani speak Arabic? On this, I was a classic American: I barely knew where Pakistan was, let alone what they spoke. But even if Eddie had talked to Christian, what did that prove? As I downed my hot sake, I decided Eddie had to be Christian's drug connection. Was there any other explanation?

After the waitress cleared the plates, Jan said: "What are you thinking about now?"

"Eddie."

"Eddie?" he said, carefully placing his chopsticks on their folded wrapper and patting his dimpled chin with a napkin. "Well, let's see," Jan continued. "Eddie's married with two boys. He lives in London . . . not all that suspicious I expect."

I laughed despite myself. I *was* leaping to conclusions. Not every Pakistani exporter dealt dope. "Okay," I said. "Let's change the subject."

"Good," Jan said, leaning back in his chair. "What about my holiday idea?" He took a long sip of sake. "Have you thought about it?"

I hadn't had the chance. But I said yes.

"Well?"

"I don't know yet." I couldn't give him an answer so soon.

"It's not an easy decision," Jan said. "You barely know me."

I knew enough about Jan to think I was falling for him. In the midst of all this chaos, I felt closer to him than ever—he was the only normal person I knew. In a city of 12 million people, I'd managed to befriend nothing but weirdoes. Once I admitted that to myself, I could also admit that I wasn't opposed to going somewhere with him. Still, I didn't tell him anything. I had to think about it a little more. He'd give me all the time I needed. That was the other thing I liked about Jan.

"Pretty soon," Jan continued, "you'll be suspecting me."

We both laughed. That was the funniest thing I'd heard yet.

While Jan dealt with the check, I headed for the bathroom. Inside, a caked-face woman was leaning over the sink blotting her chin with a powder puff. I found a swatch of mirror and studied my face, the industrial light revealing undetected bumps and fuzz. A few strands of hair had slipped from my barrette. I smoothed them back with a sprinkle of water. Smiling hard, I checked my teeth. At thirteen, when I'd finally gotten my braces off, the sight of my deluxe choppers shocked me. They seemed ridiculously enormous and white; I probably could land a job hustling dental floss.

"Want some powder?" the woman asked. From the tone of

her voice I realized she was a man in drag. It was definitely one of those nights.

"I'm okay," I said.

She snapped her compact shut and straightened the skirt that had crept up over her belly.

I applied a coat of lipstick then bit down on a tissue.

"What color is that?" She had her hip pressed against the sink.

I turned the tube over. "Scarlet Empress," I said. It was a perk left over from the Barneys gig.

"Too vicious for me," she said.

"You think?"

She nodded, still staring at me in the mirror. "Love your Pucci-esque purse."

"Thanks," I said. "I bought it in San Francisco for two bucks."

We laughed. Then she went into a pink stall and locked the door, her canoe-size satin pumps visible in the mirror. She started gagging—or something. I almost asked if she was okay, but figured it was a dumb question. I snapped my faux Pucci and gently closed the door behind me.

Back at Carmi's, we made love in our usual silent way, as Miles Davis played in the background. We'd fallen into a rhythm that was altogether different than anything I'd ever known. It was sexy and close and insular, as though the world around us had receded. I would miss our lovemaking when Jan was gone, especially his slow, deliberate touch. Now Jan was drifting off next to me, a thin arm draped across my belly, his thigh pressed against my hip. It was pleasant feeling him so near. A draught leaked in from a crack somewhere; the street was quiet for a change. I had no idea what time it was. I didn't care. Jan's steady breathing punctuated the silence. In sleep, he was as calm as he was awake. He didn't snore or toss and turn. His body was like a yogi in repose.

When the phone rang, I knew it was Kyle. It had to be: No one else called me in the middle of the night. I slipped out from under Jan's arm and wrapped myself in Carmi's robe. I glanced at the clock. It was after one thirty.

"Hello?" I said.

"Alex."

"Kyle?"

"Yeah." He coughed. "What's up?"

"What's *up?*" I said. "It's after midnight."

"I'm in the hospital."

My body went cold. "Are you sick?"

"No."

"Then what happened?"

"I got jumped."

Yassi's face suddenly appeared. "Are you hurt?"

"My arms," Kyle said. "They broke 'em . . . I can't even wipe my ass."

"Christ," I said.

"Come and see me. I'm at Saint Vincent's."

"Now?"

"I need to see you," he whispered, like he was embarrassed.

"Okay," I said. "I'll come tomorrow."

Kyle paused for a moment. The muffled fuzz of a TV coming through. ". . . I love you," he said.

"Me, too," I said, which didn't make any sense. But I wanted to make him feel better.

"Later."

The phone went dead. I stood in the dark holding the receiver. What melodrama. I would've called Yassi to tell her how prescient she'd been, but I didn't have her number; I didn't know her last name—she was probably on a plane back to Algeria. At least, I hoped she was.

When I came back to the bedroom, Jan was up. He already had his pants on. "Was that the phone?"

"Yes," I said. I felt like I was dreaming.

"You don't look well," Jan said, pausing for a second.

"I don't feel well."

He pulled his turtleneck over his head. His skin was ghostly against the charcoal-colored wool. "Who called?"

"Kyle," I said, sitting on the edge of the bed and wrapping Carmi's robe tightly around me.

Jan sat next to me. He smelled like sandalwood. He must've washed his face while I was on the phone. "What did he say?"

"He's in the hospital," I said, choking on the words. It was all turning out as Yassi had said.

"What happened now?" Jan said, screwing up his face like he couldn't believe it either.

"He got jumped."

"Jumped?"

"You know," I said. "Beat up."

"I understand," he said, threading his belt through his pant loops. "Mugged."

I didn't think he'd been mugged. If you were a mugger, you certainly wouldn't pick on Kyle. He was too big and too aware. And he didn't look like someone with money. It didn't make sense. "I don't think so," I said. "Not Kyle."

Jan frowned. "Maybe he . . . provoked someone," he said, lighting a cigarette.

"What makes you say that?"

He lightly tapped ash into a glass. "I didn't want to say anything before."

"Say what?" Now it was Jan who had something to tell me.

"That night in the bar," he said, blowing a cloud of smoke above his head, "Kyle was like a lunatic."

That was nothing new. I waited for him to continue.

"He was very . . . unpleasant." Jan took one last drag and stubbed out his cigarette. Then he slipped on his shoes.

"He's always unpleasant," I said, amazed again that the two of them had actually hung out together.

"I know," Jan said, tying a shoelace. "But he seemed so angry."

"He's always angry."

"Kyle's intent on ruining himself," he said, his eyes fixed on mine. "You can't help him."

To a degree Jan was right. Still, I felt like shit. I could've warned Kyle about Yassi and I hadn't.

Jan got up and stood in front of the mirror to comb his hair. The color was gone from his face. He seemed shaken up.

"Do you want me to stay?" he said.

"It's okay."

"Just say it."

I preferred to be alone so I could stew without interruption. Jan lingered for a while, trying to cheer me up. It was sweet of him, but I wanted to think. Finally, I walked him to the door, where he hugged me for a long time. We made plans for tomorrow, then he was gone.

I spent the rest of the night revisiting my conversations with Kyle and Yassi. I couldn't come up with anything new. The same old questions haunted me: Why was Christian dead? What did Yassi know that I didn't? Why were Kyle's arms broken? And, most important, were Kyle's broken limbs related to Christian's bad end? It was enough to keep me up until about four. I'd go see Kyle in the morning and pry the truth out of him. Even if I had to break a few bones myself.

chapter 24

The hospital stunk of ammonia, wax, and disease. The glass doors were smeared with greasy fingerprints. The halls were dingy, the linoleum peeling. The walls hadn't been painted in years. I asked a slovenly orderly for directions. She barked out Kyle's room number without making eye contact. I made my way through the place trying not to think too hard about why Kyle was here. When I finally came across his room, I stopped short: A cop was positioned outside the door. The sight of him sent my head spinning.

The cop took a noisy sip of coffee. "Yeah?" he said, his voice husky.

"I'm a friend," I said, thinking that was probably enough to get me arrested.

He shook his head.

"I know," I said. "It's hard to believe."

He laughed. It was more like a cough. "What's your name?"

"Do I have to tell you?"

"If you want in you do."

His nostrils were so huge I could practically see his brain. "Alex Orlando," I said, grabbing the door.

"Hold your horses," he said, taking a clipboard from behind a white folding chair. "Spell the last name. Slowly. And sign here."

I did. He studied the sheet for a while, as though my name held a secret clue.

"Can I go in now?"

"That an Italian name?"

I rolled my eyes. "Yes." Then I checked out his name tag: MASTRANGELO.

"I'm Italian, too." He puffed up his chest.

"Great," I said. "Can I go in?"

"Only if you tell me what a nice girl like you sees in a dirtbag like him." He jerked a thumb toward the door.

"Dirtbags appeal to me." I gave him my best smile.

He snorted and waved me in.

Kyle was watching TV; the volume was barely audible. He was propped on a bunch of pillows. His face was purple; a huge black shiner rimmed his right eye. A white bandage was taped across his forehead. His arms were braced to his chest like the wings of a roasted chicken. I winced. It looked painful. He smiled when he saw me, his face plugging in as though he'd just won the lottery. At least he hadn't lost any teeth. I pulled a chair to the bed. Nobody had sent flowers; there weren't any windows. Instead, there was a humming fluorescent light tacked by a wire to the ceiling.

"You look pretty cute in that gown," I said.

"Yeah," he said. He voice was flat, like someone had poached the volume from it. "Maybe they'll let me keep it."

I laughed.

"Yeah, I know," he said, irritably. "It's fuckin' hilarious."

"I'm sorry." It wasn't a joke.

He sighed. "Got a cigarette?"

"No," I said.

"They won't let me smoke."

"It's a hospital, not a bar."

"I don't give a fuck."

"You're awfully grouchy."

"You'd be, too, if your arms were broke."

"I'm sorry," I said, taking in his bruised hands. One eye was bloodshot, the other was swollen shut. I was ready to get to the point of my visit—how Kyle had gotten his face rearranged and whether this had anything to do with Yassi. "What happened?"

Kyle took a long breath and started to speak. "I was hangin' out at some dump near my place, talkin' to this gorgeous Cuban chick. This freak comes over and tells me to get lost, 'cause Inez—that's her name—is his wife or some shit. I told him to fuck off." Kyle settled into his mound of pillows. "He kept at it though . . . so I threw a glass of beer in his face." Kyle stopped for a minute and tried to scratch his side. "So this Inez gets all cozy with me. We're foolin' around." He smiled at the thought. "Then she's got to leave 'cause she's got to pick up her cousin or somethin'. So I pound down a few more beers, eat a tab. Then I split." He hacked a few times before getting to the inevitable climax. "Next thing I know, I got half of Havana on my back, a bunch of midgets smashin' my arms with pipes and screamin'." Kyle's voice took on a gruff tone. "I guess they knocked me out 'cause I woke up in this shithole flyin' on Demerol." He frowned. "But they shut that gravy train off after one hit."

I'd heard hundreds of similar escapades. I'd never really believed any of them. I wasn't sure I believed Kyle now.

"What about Yassi?" I said.

"What about her? I haven't seen that bitch in two weeks."

"I saw her a few days ago." I paused to watch Kyle's face. "After you dragged me to that pastry shop." But his expression didn't change.

"What'd she want?"

"She had a goddamn gun," I said, surprised at how weird I sounded. Just thinking about her irritated me. "She said I should keep my mouth shut."

"She's crazy," he said, pretending to watch TV, though the picture was obscured by static.

"You should be sorry you got me into this mess," I said.

"Sorry."

"You don't even mean it," I said. His disinterest was exasperating. "Don't you want to know what she said?"

"Not really." Kyle gave me a defeated look. It didn't make me feel any better. "What do you want me to say?"

"I don't know," I said.

"Okay," he said, sighing. "Tell me what she said."

"She said you were in trouble."

"Fuck her."

"Are you?"

"Am I what?" Kyle said, turning his good eye on me.

"In trouble?"

"I'm always in trouble."

That was a given. The question was what sort of trouble.

"But this is different," I said, feeling like a shrink.

"How?" he said.

"This trouble is . . . serious."

Kyle tried to press a button on the remote control. "Can you fuckin' change this?"

I leaned over him and flipped through the channels.

"Stop!" he shouted. Cheetahs were running across the Serengeti. "Cool," Kyle mumbled.

I was tempted to turn off the TV. "Kyle?"

"I'm right here," he said. "You don't have to scream."

"Sorry," I said. I was keyed up.

"You know," Kyle said, "male cheetahs sometimes eat their cubs."

"Fascinating."

"I should've been a vet," Kyle said, staring up at the screen wistfully.

I could just see him delivering a lamb on some back-country farm. "Yassi said something bad would happen to you."

"Something bad did happen," he said. "Look at me."

"I can see that."

"Yassi thinks she's fuckin' Nostradamus," he said. "But she doesn't know shit."

"I was supposed to warn you," I said. A wave of guilt swept over me.

Kyle laughed. "Warn me about what?"

"This."

"I told you what happened."

"I'm just trying to believe you."

He gave me a crestfallen look. "Believe me?"

"Yeah."

"What's not to believe?"

"A lot," I said.

"But I told you what went down."

"I know," I said. But that didn't explain Yassi's hysteria. Or the cop waiting outside. "What about the other day?" I said.

"What about it?"

"You said you were worried."

Kyle tried to shrug. But it was more of a jerk.

"It was the fuckin' drugs," he said.

"What drugs?"

"I don't know."

"How can you not know?"

"I huffed some shit in the morning," Kyle said. "And it wigged me out."

"What about Yassi?"

He groaned. "We're back to her again?"

"Yeah," I said. "She said you fucked with the network."

Kyle grinned. "The network?"

I nodded.

"You mean like NBC?" He laughed at himself.

"Yassi said there was a network."

"What network?" Kyle said, screwing up his purple face.

"How should I know?"

"Sounds like something out of DeLillo," he said. "Not Yassi."

"Yassi said someone did this to you because of Christian."

"I told you: Cubans did this to me," Kyle said, letting out a sigh. "Anyway, who's Christian?"

"Your dealer, remember?"

"Oh, yeah," he said, frowning. "The dead Euro."

"That Euro was Yassi's sister's boyfriend."

Kyle knitted his one good eyebrow. "Yassi doesn't have a sister."

"She said she has a sister."

"She lies like a rug."

"I saw her."

"Who?"

"Yassi's sister!" I was practically yelling.

"I told you," Kyle roared. "She doesn't have a fuckin' sister." He tried to lean forward and grimaced. "Motherfucker!"

I didn't say anything for a minute. We both stared up at the TV. The narrator was explaining how cheetahs are the fastest animals on earth, for short distances.

"She looks like Yassi," I said, my voice losing its intensity.

"What's that got to do with anything?"

"It's got to do with everything."

Kyle shook his head. "You're crazy, too."

I was beginning to think he was right. Still, I pressed on. "Yassi said you were involved."

"Involved in *what?*" he said, screwing up his face again.

"I don't know," I said. "This thing, this stuff with Christian."

"Fuck her," he said. "That bitch is just tryin' to cover her ass."

"What are *you* talking about?"

"Never mind," he said. He pursed his lips like a pouty girl.

"You must've done something pretty bad to end up like *that*." I pointed to his arms.

"No," he said. "I got beat up for scammin' pussy."

The cop was right, of course. Kyle was a dirtbag. But why the hell was there a cop outside? I wondered if Kyle could explain that.

"You know there's a cop outside."

"Yeah," he said. "He just showed up. I don't know where they think I'm runnin' off to."

"Maybe he's there to keep somebody out."

"That's bullshit," Kyle said. "They said they need me for *questioning* or some shit. A pretty-boy cop's been comin' around every few hours and grillin' me about where I've been." He paused, trying to rearrange his arms; it set him cursing like a madman. "It's nice. You get your fuckin' head kicked in and they treat you like a criminal."

A sloppy male nurse came bursting through the door. He had a limp ponytail and giant pimples. "Visiting hours are over," he said. "It's time for your sponge bath, Sunshine."

Kyle groaned. "Can't she do it?" He pointed his chin at me.

"No thanks," I said. "You're in good hands."

"Can't even get a chick nurse," Kyle said, whining.

"Sorry, honey," he said. "It's me or smell like the farm."

"I'll take the fuckin' farm," Kyle said.

The nurse went into the bathroom; I could hear water running. I said I had to go. Kyle didn't say anything. He seemed depressed, like he knew things were only going to get worse. He asked me to turn up the TV, which I did. There was a show on about mole rats. Kyle looked transfixed. "They're blind," he said, more to himself than to me. "But they can find their way around."

I said I was leaving. Kyle nodded my way and asked me to

come back soon and bring him some books. All they had in the hospital was *TV Guide* and *Fortune.*

Outside, the cop was gone. I wandered through the hospital like a zombie. I finally had to ask someone how to get out. By the time I hit the pavement, I was more confused than when I'd arrived. I trudged back to Carmi's through a cold drizzle; the streets were sticky under my boots. I tried not to think too hard about Kyle laid up in that filthy hospital. Instead I concentrated on the stately brownstones and the glistening bare trees lined up like soldiers along the streets. A faded green Christmas tree was tossed on the sidewalk—I wondered who'd wait till February to get rid of their tree. It was sort of beautiful—the only thing half-alive on this gray day.

chapter 25

Back at Carmi's, I checked my messages. A bunch of hangups that made me queasy and a message from Malcolm. I stood over the machine and listened to his rabid voice. Evidently, a detective had come to see him at Barneys and chased his customers away. Malcolm didn't mind so much because the cop was actually quite a looker—if you fancied the well-groomed macho type. Malcolm wasn't sure what he wanted; he'd asked a lot of vague questions about where he'd been on a certain night and what he was writing—were they thinking of hiring him for a copper consultantship? He'd tell me more over lunch at Kaps, a greasy spoon across the street from Barneys. I was to meet him day after tomorrow at one o'clock sharp. "Remember," he said, "your time is your word." It occurred to me that Malcolm might throw a tantrum about the fact that I still hadn't been able to locate his play.

I knew the interrogation had something to do with Christian. It made me think twice about Malcolm. I didn't know him as well as I thought I did. I wondered if I should see him again. Maybe Malcolm was a suspect.

I stepped into the kitchen to make myself dinner. When I returned to the living room with my tuna melt, I got the shock of my life. Yassi and some fat man I'd never seen before were planted on Carmi's couch. They must've followed me in. I was sure I'd closed the door behind me—at least I thought I had—not that it mattered now. So much for Carmi's double-lock theory. If Yassi knew how to shoot people, I guess she knew how to break into apartments. I stood under the door jamb—my first impulse was to run back into Carmi's room and call the police—but the bedroom door didn't shut. I was stuck. Yassi was back to finish me off. I was sure of it. Panic shot through my limbs. I heard myself tell them to get the fuck out . . . it was ballsy, but I said it.

Yassi didn't move. She looked exactly the same except for a pair of giant aviator glasses that obscured her eyes. "I didn't want to come here," she said, rubbing her bony hands together.

That made two of us. "You didn't have to."

"But I did."

I waited to hear her reason. "Sit down," she said, motioning toward Carmi's chair with her papery hand. I did as I was told. For the first time, I took in the gargantuan next to her. He had sprouts of curly black hair coming from every place except his head. He must've weighed close to three hundred pounds. A human hairy blob. He was sweating; giants beads collected on his upper lip.

"It's about a *play,*" she continued.

"A play?" I repeated. We had officially stepped into the twilight zone. I wondered if she had her gun . . . I wondered if it had a silencer . . . I couldn't think. "What play?"

"There's only one," she yelped, hopping off the couch. My heart skipped a beat. I'd have to pretend—I pointed to Carmi's bookshelf. "There are a few plays over there." Carmi had a pretty impressive Tennessee Williams collection. I didn't know why I remembered. I'd noticed it my first night.

Yassi was on them in a second, tilting her head so she could read the spines. "Bourgeois shit," she grumbled. What did she expect, Bertolt Brecht? The fat man just sat there immobile, his breathing labored like he was about to pass out. Maybe he was having a heart attack. In his right hand was a tiny pistol, like a water gun, really, clenched between flabby rolls. I thought I might be seeing things.

Yassi started yanking out books—some plays and some not—and leafing through the pages. I didn't bother to point out the difference.

"It's not here," she shouted, giving me a suspicious look. Her bald head flushed pink. "Give me what I want, okay?"

"I'm trying," I mumbled. I looked at the fat man, hoping for a little sympathy. But he had his eyes closed. Then it dawned on me. Could she mean Malcolm? Hadn't the cops asked him about his work at Barneys? It was worth a try. "You mean *Kitty Kats and Kleptomaniacs?*" I said.

"What are you talking about!?" She was still yelling. I hoped someone would hear—maybe I'd be saved from this after all.

"Hold on," I said. I stood up carefully. I was sure they were about to kill me. I nodded toward the bedroom. Yassi and the fat man didn't seem worried that I'd run away or call the cops. There wasn't anywhere to go, besides the window—a sixteen-story drop to the street. I went into the bedroom to pretend to retrieve Malcolm's play. I still had no idea where it was. Imagine getting killed over a lost manuscript. That's what I was thinking as I rummaged through Carmi's nightstand, the last place I'd seen Malcolm's play. I hoped I'd overlooked it. Except it wasn't there. I felt the panic rushing back like an epileptic fit. In the other room, I heard Yassi talking Arabic or Algerian or whatever the fuck it was to the fat man. Next thing I knew, she was standing beside me while I riffled through a stack of books.

"So where is it?" she said, pulling the pillows off the bed. Now her tone was calm. She frowned. "I need that play."

I wasn't ready to admit I couldn't find it. Would they kill me if I couldn't? Did that make any sense? Ten minutes later, the room looked as though a cyclone had hit it. Pillows were on the floor. Magazines were tossed off the shelves. Drawers hung open. The play was gone . . .

Yassi surveyed the place, hands on her hips like a demented drill sergeant. She stalked around the apartment, slamming cabinets and drawers. "What did you do with it?" she demanded.

"I didn't do anything with it," I said.

"Did you bring it to Christian's?" she said.

"I never even went to Christian's."

Suddenly, her eyes widened. "Fuck," she said, snapping her fingers. "Giti said Christian had the play." She was talking to herself now. "She said he gave it back to you."

I couldn't imagine why. Christian hadn't been *much for the reading.* Only three people had been in the apartment: Christian, Kyle, and Jan. That meant one of them must've nicked it. *Why?*—I had no idea. The bastards.

"You better find that suckin' play," she said. We were back in the living room. The fat man was snoring. Yassi smacked him and said something clipped and guttural. He opened his eyes and looked blankly at me like he didn't know where he was. He let out a long groan as he pushed himself off the couch. He slipped the little pistol into a jacket pocket.

Yassi got in my face one last time. "We'll be back," she said. And with that, they were gone.

I followed Carmi's orders to a tee. I locked every bolt behind them *and* latched the chain, my hands shaking. I made my way back to the couch and flopped on the center cushion. The fat man had left a rank odor, like gym socks. I got up and opened a window. I still couldn't believe Yassi had broken in; she'd probably been following me. I felt like hopping right back on a plane to California, where at least I felt safe and sane. If it wasn't for Carmi, I would've been gone days ago. I thought about calling the cops. But what would I say? Had I been threatened? I guess I had. I felt like I had. I didn't want to implicate myself . . . I didn't want to be involved. But what was I involved in? I kept thinking this whole thing would blow over soon enough. Why had Yassi said she'd be back? I hoped I'd be gone by the time she got round to it. And if she'd wanted to get rid of me, she just had the perfect opportunity. Didn't she?

I couldn't comprehend why Yassi wanted Malcolm's play. Did *they* know one another? Was I missing something? Anything seemed plausible now. I decided to call Malcolm. I wasn't sure what I was going to ask him . . .

"*Pronto,*" he said.

"Malcolm?"

"Who else?"

"It's Alex."

"How are you, my dear?"

"Fine," I said.

"You don't sound fine."

I sighed. "It's a long story."

"That old clichè."

"Yeah," I said, changing the subject. "Listen, do you know a Yassi?"

"Yassi?" he repeated, like he was speaking another language. "Sounds like a falafel."

"It's a person," I said. "A woman."

"Then no," he said. "But I know a Falassi. She's a he though, and a damn good actress."

"Great," I said, wondering if I should believe him. Lately, I didn't believe anyone. Though Malcolm hadn't missed a beat when I mentioned Yassi's name.

"Is that all?" he said.

"I guess."

"Is this Yassi interested in my work?" Malcolm said.

"Actually, she is," I said.

"Well, tell her to call my agent. Got a pen?"

"Yes," I said, even though I didn't.

"What selections?"

"Kitty Kats—"

"That dreck?"

"It's genius, remember?"

"Yes, I know." He sighed. "I have a few extra copies for the Pulitzer committee."

I suddenly remembered the way he'd claimed to only have one copy. I reminded Malcolm of his tantrum, catching him in a lie.

"Oh, that," he said, recovering quickly. "I always make five copies of everything I write—you remember what happened to Hemingway."

"But you said . . ."

"I know, I know," he said. "I had to make a point."

I almost asked him what the point was. But in light of everything it didn't seem that important.

"Well, it's back to my scribbling now," he said. "You know how it is."

I didn't but I said I did.

"See you at Kaps?"

"Oh," I said, sort of nonchalantly. "I can't make it."

"Why not?" he demanded.

I wasn't quick enough with my answer.

"You don't want to see me," he huffed, his voice taking on the same bitter tone as when he'd accused me of not reading his play. "That's just fine."

"Wait," I said, not wanting to listen to one of his tirades. "I'll try to . . . rearrange things." I didn't sound very convincing.

"Well," he snapped. "See you there."

"Alright," I said, thinking I could just blow him off. But I was genetically incapable of being rude.

"Cheers then."

"Right back at you," I said. But he'd already hung up.

I stood there holding the receiver, wondering if Malcolm was involved in this weird plot. It didn't seem beyond the realm of possibility. Again, Malcolm's interminably red runny nose came back to me. That, and the fact that he'd practically admitted to swapping leather jackets for a few lines of coke. Perhaps Malcolm's interest in human brutality wasn't altogether literary.

chapter 26

As planned, Jan came over later that night. While we drank a bottle of wine, I described the afternoon's festivities, beginning with my trip to see Kyle and ending with Yassi's surprise visit. Jan listened in his careful, quiet way; nothing I said seemed to surprise him. Occasionally, he'd ask a simple question. By the time I was finished, he was deep in thought, watching the burgundy swirl around his glass. Then he said: "This is becoming insane."

Becoming. It already was.

"You can't speak to Kyle anymore," Jan continued. "I don't trust him or his friends."

As usual, Jan was right. I didn't much like Kyle these days let alone trust him, and I definitely didn't care for his friends.

"What bothers me," Jan said, "is that this play just disappeared." He glanced around the apartment. "That means someone else was here—either with you or without you."

That bothered me. If Yassi could follow me to Carmi's and let herself in with some thug, anyone could've come and gone without my knowledge. Paranoia got the better of me. "I'm worried about getting myself killed."

"I don't think you have to be concerned about that," Jan said.

"How do you know?"

"It doesn't make any sense."

Nothing made sense lately.

"Did you call the police?" Jan continued, wrapping his arm around me.

"No."

"I don't know if you should," he said, as he distractedly rubbed my arm.

"Because Yassi said not to?"

"No," Jan said. "Because I don't want you to get involved in this."

"I already am."

"That's what I'm afraid of."

I didn't have to think too long about whether to go to the cops or not.

Just as we were deciding on where to have dinner, the doorbell rang. I wasn't expecting anyone and I thought with a chill that it might be Yassi. Jan wanted to answer the door for me; instead, I made him stand beside me. Then I said: "Who is it?" The voice on the other side said: "Police." I wasn't sure I believed him. I looked at Jan. He latched the chain and I opened the door a crack.

I did a double take. It was Jacob, the party promoter from the airport. He flipped me his badge as my mouth flapped open. "Police," he said, again. This time with a wink. "Mind if I ask you a few questions?" Mute, I shook my head. Everything was becoming ridiculous; I half-expected Christian to come traipsing out of the bedroom to declare the whole thing *a very funny trick—you are liking tricks, no?*

"I'm not really a party promoter," Jacob said.

"Really?" I quickly sized him up again. He looked exactly the same. Black curly hair, olive skin, baby cheeks, and smart dark eyes. Was he Kyle's pretty-boy cop?

"Alex 'Candy' Orlando?" he said.

I smiled. I'd forgotten about that.

Detective Jacob Bloom introduced himself.

"We gave our statements to the police," Jan said, trying to be helpful.

"I know," Jacob said, glancing his way. "I just need a little more info." He smiled, showing off a set of healthy teeth. Somehow, we all ended up in Carmi's kitchen. We'd followed Jacob. He was like that—a sort of tacit leader. We gathered around the 1950s dinette table; I felt like I was on trial.

"Nice place you got here," Jacob said, his eyes roaming over the kitchen.

"It's my uncle's," I said.

"That would be . . . " Jacob said, flipping through his black note pad, "Anthony Carmine Orlando."

"Yes," I said. "Carmi." My poor uncle. All these people trespassing through his palace.

Jacob scooted in his chair. He tapped the linoleum with his loafer.

"I want to confirm again what time you left Hangerman," Jacob said, staring across the table at Jan. He was referring to Kyle, of course, which I explained for Jan's sake.

"Like I said," Jan said, "we parted around half-past eleven. But I can't be sure."

"That gives him plenty of time," Jacob said, glancing at his watch as if to confirm.

"Gives *who* plenty of time?" I said, even though I knew. I waited to hear Jacob say it out loud. That'd make it real—or more accurately—surreal.

"Hangerman, Kyle. He had just enough time to get back here . . . and whack Olsen."

I tried to process what I was hearing. Despite all his posing, Kyle wasn't capable of killing anyone, Christian included. He was a coward at heart. "What would Kyle have against Christian?" I said.

Jacob shrugged. This was an everyday thing for him. "Maybe Olsen stiffed him on a deal."

I shook my head. Kyle wouldn't kill someone over a bag of dope. "It can't be."

"Olsen was involved with quite a few sketchy people," Jacob said. "We've been following him—and his 'friends'—for three months."

I wondered if Jacob had been following me at the airport. After all, I was one of Christian's friends. He gave me a slight nod like he read my mind.

Jan shook his head as though the whole thing was still unbelievable to him.

"Do you know a Yassi Ahmet?" Jacob said.

"Not exactly," I said. I was about to tell him about her visit, but he cut me off.

"We know she was just here," he said, leaning back in his chair. "We know all about her."

Then why ask? And why hadn't they come up here and dragged her off to jail for breaking and entering? . . .

"It's all right," he said, with a wave of his hand. "She's got a few critics at the ATF. Guns and smack, mostly. Barroom brawls . . . over her *anarchist* views." Jacob smirked. "No murders or maimings to date . . . and don't worry about that whale she pals around with. He's her cousin. A chiropractor in Queens."

If he was trying to make me feel better, it really wasn't working. I could tell by the way he was watching me, the way his eyes sparkled. He seemed to know everything.

"The dent in Olsen's head," Jacob rattled on matter-of-factly. "The ruptured meningeal artery indicates someone pretty strong." He unbuttoned his trench coat; he'd never bothered to take it off. I assumed that meant he wasn't staying long. "One other thing," Jacob said. "We found a manuscript in Olsen's apartment, by some guy . . ." He flipped through his notebook again. "Foxman. Malcolm. A play. *Kit Kats* and something. Pretty funny stuff."

So that's where it had gone. Yassi was right for a second time. Christian must've taken it, though *that* hardly made sense. "I worked with Malcolm at Barneys."

"We know," Jacob said. "We brought Foxman in for questioning."

"That must've been interesting," I said, choking out a laugh. I already knew they'd talked to him. Jacob was obviously the "looker" Malcolm had mentioned. But hearing it from Jacob made me wonder even more about Malcolm.

"You could say that," Jacob said, grinning. "Says he loaned you the play, and you lost it."

"I didn't lose it," I said. "It disappeared."

"It had Hangerman's handwriting in the margins," Jacob said. "A kind of running commentary, like he was a critic."

It was getting weirder by the moment. Kyle, a drama critic? A drama queen was more like it. Of course, I couldn't explain what the hell Kyle's handwriting was doing in the margins. I guess that proved Kyle did know Christian—or Malcolm—or both. Why they'd be sharing a play was beyond me. It wasn't like they'd formed a book club.

"When did you notice the play was missing?" Jacob said.

"I don't remember," I said. I figured it was better than saying I never really knew it was gone.

"That's not good enough," Jacob said.

"What do you want me to say?" Christian had stopped by so many times I could hardly pinpoint the exact date he'd ripped it off. I didn't want to get into specifics with Jan sitting next to me.

"She doesn't know," Jan said, like he was bored by Jacob's questions. It was nice having him on my side.

Jacob ignored him. "We found Kyle's prints all over Olsen's apartment," he continued. "We found a set on his toothbrush. You want to tell me exactly how often those two were together?"

I didn't offer anything because I didn't know.

"We know you were pretty chummy with Olsen," Jacob said, giving Jan a sidelong glance. "We know all about that."

I had an image of Christian and me caught on grainy black-and-white photos splashed with coffee on some copper's desk.

"I've already told you what I know," I said. "What do you want?"

"Alex," Jan said, cutting in with a firm hand on my shoulder. "You're getting upset for no reason." He looked at Jacob. "What else can she possibly tell you?"

"Would you mind giving us a few minutes—alone," Jacob said, as though he didn't have the time to deal with Jan.

It was more a statement than a question. Jan shook his head like he couldn't comprehend what was going on around him. "I was just leaving," he said, his voice taking on a steely edge. It was the first time I'd seen Jan mad. He squeezed my shoulder and took his time vacating the kitchen. He poked his head into the refrigerator and grabbed a couple of oranges. Jacob scowled at him. "I'll call you later," Jan said to me. He kissed me on the cheek. Then he left us in the kitchen. I'd lost my defense. I felt like a quarterback about to get sacked.

When Jacob heard the door shut, he said: "Now, tell me what you know about the play."

"Malcolm lent it to me. I read it and kept forgetting to give it back. Then it disappeared. "

"Why would Christian want it?"

"I have no idea," I said. "It was just a play."

"Maybe not."

"What do you mean?"

"Never mind," Jacob said. "What did Ahmet say?"

"You mean Yassi?"

He nodded impatiently.

"She wanted the play—"

"Right. I already had a little chat with her," he said, with a wink. "You won't be seeing her anymore."

I hoped he was right.

"When did Foxman give it to you?" Jacob said.

"I don't know," I said. "Maybe three or four weeks ago?"

"Three or four weeks," Jacob said, rolling his eyes. "That guy's got a memory like a sieve. He says you took the play two *months* ago."

Leave it to Malcolm.

"Ever see Foxman with Olsen?"

"Once," I said, recalling their chance meeting. "At Barneys."

Jacob perked up at this. "What happened?"

I shook my head. "Nothing."

"What'd they talk about?"

I tried to remember. It was a blur now. "Malcolm wanted to know if Christian knew his work."

"And?"

"He didn't."

"Anything else?"

"Yeah," I said. "Malcolm kept calling Christian a Nazi."

"Was he?"

"A Nazi?" I said, holding back a laugh.

Jacob smiled, quick and bright.

"No," I said. "That much I'm sure of."

Jacob scribbled something in his black notebook. Then he looked up at me. "Foxman didn't threaten him, did he?"

"No," I said, wondering what he was getting at now. "What are you saying?"

"Nothing," Jacob said. "Only Foxman has been known to get pretty wild with a tote bag." He allowed himself a clipped chuckle.

"A tote bag?" I said.

Jacob nodded. "Couple of years ago. Went berserk at Saks," he said, rapidly. "Smacked someone with this giant bag . . ."

I imagined Malcolm violently wielding a Louis Vuitton tote. It was pretty funny. Disturbing, too. I was about to ask Jacob to elaborate but he'd already moved on.

"What about Foxman and Hangerman—they ever hang out?"

I recalled how much Malcolm had despised Kyle. "They met once. Also at Barneys."

Jacob noted this.

"Tell me about your time with Olsen," he said, moving on. "Who you saw him with, who he called, where he went."

"There's nothing to tell," I said. "We had dinner once or twice. He took me to his gym. I never saw him with anyone except his ex-girlfriend—Yassi's sister."

"We already know about her," Jacob said. "She got married last week in Algeria."

"Sorry," I said.

"What about phone calls? Any strange ones?"

"He was supposedly getting calls from Pakistan, about some . . . rugs."

Jacob nodded slowly. "For his 'architectural' projects?"

"Yes," I said, thinking how ridiculous it sounded.

"Did you know Olsen dropped out of Columbia's architecture program?"

I shook my head. So much for the Columbia.

"He did a couple of cool kitchens down in Tribeca," Jacob said, thoughtfully touching his pencil to his chin.

At least he hadn't lied about one thing. It was somehow comforting.

Jacob chortled. "So what about these calls?"

"What about them," I said. "Christian spoke Swedish or pigeon Arabic. I didn't understand a word."

"Then how did you know he was talking to Pakistan?"

"Because that's what he said."

the foreigner_____**MEG CASTALDO**

149

"They don't speak Arabic in Pakistan," Jacob said, another smile brightening his face.

"Then what do they speak?"

"Urdu."

"Maybe he was speaking Urdu," I said, shrugging. "I wouldn't know."

"And you, of course, believed him?"

"Not exactly," I said.

"Ever meet any *rug* dealer?"

I shook my head. "Just an exporter."

"Oh yeah," said Jacob, flipping through his black notebook. "Eddie Nazir?"

I nodded. Was there anything he didn't know?

"Yeah," Jacob said. "We're checking on him."

So Eddie might've been lying. I tried to gleam something from Jacob's face. But he didn't give anything away. He was probably a great poker player.

"Did you ever see Olsen with Hangerman?"

"No," I said. "I told you. I didn't know they knew each other until after . . . Christian died."

"You find that odd?"

"Very."

"Did Hangerman ever say anything about him to you?"

"Not really."

"Was he jealous?"

"Of Christian?"

Jacob nodded. He leaned across the table, watching me intently. I felt myself blushing—something that hardly ever happened to me.

"He said he was, but . . ."

"Did you find that weird?"

"Not really," I said. "Kyle's jealous of everyone." As soon as I said that, I wanted to take it back. It sounded all wrong.

"We know about his rap sheet. Mostly baby stuff."

I nodded. I wasn't telling Jacob anything new. Still, he was probably holding back on me.

"How long have you known him?" he said, giving me a hard look.

"Eleven years."

"Ever threaten you?"

"No."

"Ever threaten anyone you knew?"

"No," I said, hesitating. Kyle was always ranting about some-one, but that was just Kyle. It was in his genes. There wasn't any other way to describe it.

"You don't seem too sure."

"Well," I said, feeling compelled to tell the truth. "Sort of."

"Sort of what?"

"You know," I said. "It's just Kyle."

"Sorry," he said, shaking his head. "I don't."

"Kyle talks a lot."

"About?"

"About what he's gonna do."

"For example?"

"I don't know," I sighed. "Stupid stuff . . ."

"Like?"

"Like," I said, "stuff I don't believe."

"But I might."

"Might what?" I said.

"Believe it. Believe the stuff."

"But you shouldn't," I said.

"Why not?"

"Because Kyle's full of himself."

"Full of himself how?"

"He makes . . . *pronouncements.*"

"Tell me," Jacob said, leaning into my space even more. I could smell the tinge of peppermint on his breath. "Did he ever make a pronouncement about Olsen?"

I nodded slowly. I couldn't turn back now.

"What was it?"

"He said he'd hurt Christian if he ever hurt me."

Jacob leaned forward. "Did you believe him?"

"No," I said. "Do you?"

"That depends," Jacob said.

"On what?"

"On the possibility of someone else making that same pronouncement." Jacob flopped against the back of the chair.

I felt like a murderer myself—like I'd stabbed Kyle a dozen times in the back. I rubbed my face. It felt numb. "So you think it was Kyle?" I said.

"Hard to say," he said, smoothing back his curls. "I'm not arresting him, if that's what you mean. Not yet, at least. Meanwhile, I got a man outside his door."

I nodded. So that's why there was a cop at the hospital.

"I'm sorry," he said.

"Thanks."

"Not about Hangerman."

"About what then?"

"Having to upset you."

It was nice of him to pretend he cared. "I'm fine."

He nodded. "You remember anything else," he said, "call me." He was up and at the door in an instant.

"Wait," I said.

He had his hand on the door knob. "Yeah?"

"What were you doing at the airport?"

"Working," he said.

"Why did you talk to me?"

"Why do you think?" He was smiling. I was amusing to him.

"You were watching me. Because of Christian?"

He shook his head. "Not exactly."

"Then what?"

"Sorry," he said. "It's confidential." He opened the door. "And one more thing." He paused to look at the Turkish plates in Carmi's foyer. "I hate to say this but . . . don't leave town."

After Jacob left, I finished the bottle of wine that Jan and I had started while brooding over the things I'd just told Jacob. I guess I was already feeling guilty. The way Jacob phrased his questions . . . the look on his face. They'd all conspired to make me tell everything I knew about Kyle—good and bad, all those over-the-top details I'd never taken seriously. Now I felt like I'd buried him. I kept reminding myself that it wasn't my fault. If Kyle hadn't been so careless in the first place—if he'd minded his own business and used his head for once in his life—none of this would've come to pass. And I still didn't know the extent of his involvement. I kept hoping it was nothing more than a bunch of coincidences. There were plenty of other shady people to check up on.

Jan called me pretty late. I was just on the verge of falling asleep. We didn't talk long. He wanted to make sure that I was okay, that the cop hadn't disturbed me. It sounded like he was in a bar; I could hear the din of voices and music in the background. When we said our good-nights, I could've sworn he told me he loved me. Or maybe I was already dreaming.

chapter 27

I dragged myself out of bed the next morning and headed straight back to the hospital. Maybe it was guilt for what I'd told Jacob. Or maybe, like Jan said, I was becoming obsessed. I had a nagging suspicion that I was missing something. I'd get Kyle to tell me the truth, even if it took all day. I wanted to lash into him about Yassi. He hadn't told me she was psychotic. When I got to his room, there was a different cop in the hallway. He didn't bother to sign me in. He barely glanced at me. He was too engrossed in a crossword puzzle.

Kyle was propped on a bunch of pillows, a book against his pointy knees. He looked better. The swelling around his eyes had subsided. The black-and-blues were beginning to fade. He was definitely on the mend. He gave me a sour smile as I pulled up a chair. I said: "Hi, honey, I'm home."

"Yeah," he said, peering over his book. "I was sure you'd left me for good."

I almost said I was sure, too. But I wanted to start off on a decent note. I'd brought him three books from Carmi's collection. "Here," I said, dropping them on the bed. "For your reading pleasure."

Kyle scanned the titles. "This shit is all Japanese."

"I know," I said. "But it's in English."

Kyle frowned. "Couldn't you have at least brought me something cool?"

"Give it a chance," I said.

"You give it a chance."

"I already have." I didn't tell Kyle that I hadn't liked them much.

"Put 'em in there," he motioned toward a skinny cabinet with his nose. Inside, there were more obscure books, odder than the ones I'd brought.

"The last guy in here died," Kyle said.

"That's comforting," I said.

Most of the books were translated from Serbo-Croatian.

"No one ever came to get them."

"Lucky you," I said.

"He was a professor."

"I can tell."

"He got cancer," Kyle said.

"How do you know?"

"The nurse."

"Oh," I said, not really wanting to hear the details.

I took a seat next to the bed. I wasn't in the mood for small talk. "Yassi followed me to Carmi's and broke in," I said. "With some fat guy."

"You mean Ari?" he said, squinting at me. "Her cousin?"

"I don't know who he was," I said. "But he had a gun."

"That dude stinks," Kyle said, giggling. "Like ass."

"I don't care," I said. "Are you listening to me?"

Kyle sighed. "Yeah," he said. "I'm listenin'."

"Well?"

"Well what?" he said. "I told you: Yassi's fucked up. But she won't hurt you. She just acts big."

Acts big. I could tell I wasn't going to get anything from Kyle. It was out of his hands now.

"Stay away from her," Kyle said, yawning.

"She should stay away from me," I said. He was beginning to irritate me. "Why don't you tell her that?"

"I would," Kyle said. "If she'd ever come and see me." He frowned.

"Speaking of visits," I said. "A cop dropped in on me."

"So?" he said.

"He asked me a bunch of questions about you."

"Like what?"

"Like if you had any grudges against anyone."

"Grudges?"

I nodded. It was the first thing that came to mind.

"I hope you told him yes," he said, grinning.

I had. But I didn't tell Kyle.

"They've got nothin' on me," he said. "Otherwise they would've arrested me by now."

"Don't be so sure."

"I am sure," he said, as though he was insulted.

"You should be more accommodating," I said. "Clear things up."

"I have been," he said. "I don't know what they expect me to say."

"Tell them the truth."

"I did," he groaned.

"Then there shouldn't be any hassle."

"If there is," Kyle said, "I'm gettin' a lawyer."

For whatever reason, this seemed an admission of guilt.

"Do you know any?" Kyle said.

"What?"

"Lawyers."

"No," I said.

Kyle stared at me for a minute; he looked like he was on the verge of telling me something, his lips slightly parted. He changed his mind in a flash, pretending to read his book: *The Life of Balzac.*

"You know," he said. "This is pretty good."

"What?"

"This Balzac dude," Kyle said. "He drank about a hundred cups of coffee a day."

"I know," I said. "Everybody knows that." But Kyle wasn't listening. He was trying to turn a page with his pinkie finger. I didn't make a move to help him.

"I want to know what you wrote on Malcolm Foxman's play."

"Who's Malcolm Foxman?" he said, giving up on the book and straightening his legs.

"A playwright."

"A playwright?" Kyle said, screwing up his face like he didn't understand.

"Yes."

"Is he famous?"

"He thinks so," I said.

"What'd he write?"

"A lot of stuff."

"Never heard of him," Kyle said with a huff.

"You just don't remember."

"Then remind me."

"Kitty Kats and Kleptomaniacs, by Malcolm Foxman."

Kyle shook his head.

"You read it," I said. "At Christian's."

"Who's Christian?"

I groaned. "Don't start the Abbott and Costello routine with me."

"I swear," he said. "I'm not."

"Christian is the dead Euro, remember?" I said. "Your dealer?"

"Oh, him," Kyle said.

"Yeah, him."

"Then who's this writer guy I'm supposed to know."

"You met him once at Barneys," I said. "You read his play."

"Is it about some angels or somethin'?"

"Yeah," I said.

"Oh," he said. "That."

I waited. Kyle rearranged his arms. Then he told me how he'd come to write on Malcolm's play.

Apparently, Kyle had been hanging out at Christian's one evening, getting stoned. "I was bored," he said. "He didn't have any books." Kyle craned his neck so he could look at me. "I don't get why you liked that Euro in the first place—the guy was a lightweight." Kyle pulled the covers up to his chin with his teeth. "Anyway, I found this play, started readin' it, and ended up nickin' it. I underlined shit I liked. He had this funny thing about gettin' revenge on anyone who crossed you. I liked that part the best." He let out a laugh. "That was pretty cool."

It seemed like a plausible explanation though I knew I'd never find out why Christian had stolen it in the first place. "Then what happened?"

"Nothin'," Kyle said. "I don't know why everyone's making a big deal over some play by some small-time Genet."

"A lot of people want that play," I said.

"Who?"

"Yassi, for one," I said.

He looked like he was about to cry. "I'm all fucked up in the hospital and she's worried about some stupid goddamn play?"

"The cops have it now," I said. "They wanted it, too."

"I know," he said. "Maybe they can stage it." He laughed at himself.

"What about Christian, then?" I said. "How'd the play get back to him?"

Kyle sighed like I was boring him. "Christian was flipped out about it," he said. "He gave me a free bag of shitty weed just for bringing it back. Okay? You convinced?"

"I guess," I said, but I wasn't. I thought he was lying.

"Did you like it?" Kyle said.

"The play?"

"Yeah," he said. "I thought it was funny."

"Me, too."

At least we agreed on one thing.

When I got back to Carmi's, Jacob was in the lobby talking to Louis, the doorman. When he saw me, he grinned and said there were a few more things he had to know. Would I mind having a quick chat? We could walk around the block. That's all it'd take. What could I say? I had nothing to hide. Outside, a cold glaring sun had finally emerged. It was a cruel joke to my California skin. We walked silently to the corner. I didn't want to circle the block twice, so I asked him what was on his mind.

"Oh," he said. "Nothing, really."

"That's a twist," I said. "You're usually full of questions."

Jacob smiled at this and stepped off the curb. Traffic came bearing down on us; a cabby leaned heavy on his horn. Jacob flipped him off.

"Don't do that," I said.

"Sorry," he said. "I hate to wait."

That was obvious. But at least he had the sense to apologize.

"So here's what I want to know," he continued, giving me a sidelong glance, his cheeks ruddy. "This play that you lost, that Foxman authored, that Olsen found, that Hangerman scribbled on? Well, it had a *directive* on it."

"A directive?" What was a directive? I didn't bother asking. I knew he'd tell me.

"Directions," he said. "You know, like, turn right on Mulberry, turn left on Canal." Jacob stopped to peer into a bakery window. "Coffee?" he said.

"Sure," I said. We went inside. The place was so overheated I immediately began to perspire.

"Sit," he said, nodding at a few stools lined up by the window. I sat while Jacob got the coffee.

"Here," he said, handing me a steaming mug.

"Thanks," I said.

"I know this is a drag," he said, sitting down and unbuttoning his jacket. "Hangin' around the likes of me."

It wasn't so terrible. But I didn't tell him that.

"You've been really helpful," he said.

"I'm trying."

He sipped his coffee, made a face, and dropped in three sugar cubes.

"You just come from the hospital?"

There wasn't any point in answering. As always, he already knew.

"I wouldn't do that," he said, "if I were you. You know, guilt by association."

I had my coat off but I was still sweating. "I didn't do anything," I said.

"I know," he said, "but people might not agree."

"What people?"

"I'm not sure."

"That's not very comforting," I said.

"I got a man on your building. You'll be fine."

He was scaring me. A man on my building? Where?

"Standard procedure," he said. "Don't look so freaked out."

Standard procedure. I nodded. Carmi didn't have a rule about dealing with a surveillance team. Did that mean I had to shove a chair under the door knob or sleep with one eye open?

"Now let's get back to this play," he said.

"Fine."

"The directions were in Swedish. We got it translated by some professor at Hunter."

"What did it say?"

"Sorry," he said. "I can't tell you."

Irritated, I asked him again, but Jacob just slid off his stool.

"You're leaving already?" I said.

"That's enough, for now."

He'd hardly asked me anything.

Jacob was already walking away. "I got a lot of dead bodies piling up on my desk." He pushed the glass door open. "By the way," he said, looking down. "Nice shoes."

I smiled. They were the shoes Christian had given me. I wondered if Jacob knew about that, too. I watched as he flew down the street, his long coat blowing in the wind behind him. He was gone in a flash. I hadn't even finished half my coffee. Jacob's cup was empty. He was the fastest guy I'd ever met. I hoped that quality found its way into his work.

chapter 28

I was supposed to meet Malcolm at Kaps. After what I'd heard from Jacob, I decided that I would blow him off. After all, I felt like I hardly knew Malcolm. And I'd misjudged enough people already. Still, I was haunted by the image of my neurotic former colleague, chain-smoking in his tattered vinyl booth and looking forlornly at the entrance every time the door swung open. It bothered me all morning. I ended up feeling so bad that I dressed for the Arctic weather and trudged over to Kaps. I reminded myself it was midday. The place was always crowded.

By the time I sunk into the booth, Malcolm already had his lunch in front of him, though he'd respectfully refrained from digging in. He always ordered the same thing: two hard-boiled eggs and a scoop of cottage cheese with plenty of pepper on a bed of iceberg lettuce. He said his ascetic nature required such a diet. That, and the fact that his mother had raised him on hot dogs and buttered macaroni.

"You're late," Malcolm said with a sniffle.

We'd said one o'clock. I glanced at my watch. It was 1:14. That hardly qualified as late in my book. But I didn't argue. Arguing with Malcolm was like trying to climb Mount Everest. You never got to the top.

"But that's okay," he said, cracking a smile. "You're not obscenely late."

I wondered what obscenely late was in Malcolm's cosmology. "Sorry," I said. "I couldn't decide what to wear."

Malcolm gagged out a laugh.

A waitress with a golden bleach job shuffled by. I ordered grilled cheese and a cup of tomato soup—both seemed pretty safe.

"How are things at the farm?" I said.

"Oh, status quo."

"Surviving then?"

"You know me," he said.

"Still ruling the roost?"

"Nobody cuts in on my territory," Malcolm said, fiddling with his knife.

I couldn't help but wonder if he was referring to something beyond Barneys.

The waitress dumped off my lunch. Malcolm snatched the pepper and shook it furiously until everything was dusted in a sooty blanket. "They never get it right," he said. "It's the pepper that makes this dish so delicioso."

"Ah, the pepper," I said. "I thought it was the iceberg."

Malcolm rolled his eyes, a white curd of cheese stuck to his chin.

"So?" he said, brightly. "How are *you?*"

"Okay," I said. I couldn't think of anything else to say. I wanted to ask Malcolm why the cops had wanted to talk to him. But he brought it up first.

"I guess you heard I got *frisked,*" he said, snickering.

"I heard."

"But the cops are such dolts," he said, flailing his arms for the waitress. When she creaked by, he ordered two coffees for himself and one for me, even though I'd barely started eating. "They can't get anything straight . . ."

"What do you mean?"

"Oh, you know," he said, scanning the room. "They asked about *my* past. But they hardly had the right story . . ."

The right story. "What story?"

"My brush with the law . . ."

So Jacob hadn't been kidding. I waited, but Malcolm didn't elaborate. He excused himself and went to the bathroom. When he returned, I could swear his nose was three shades redder. Or maybe it was my imagination. It was hard to say.

The waitress delivered the coffees. I took a sip. It tasted like the bottom of the pot. A few chalky grounds floated to the top.

"Did you know that beast of yours deigned to critique my play?" Malcolm said, bristling like a skunk ready to shoot off its stench.

The "beast" could only be Kyle. "Kyle, you mean?"

Malcolm snorted. "Remember when he came to Barneys looking for you?"

"Oh, yeah."

"He was such a Neanderthal," Malcolm said, shaking his head. "I was surprised that he showed a keen interest in my work, though I know how compelling I can be—even to a *dummkopf.*"

I didn't bother defending Kyle. There wasn't any point in trying to convince Malcolm of Kyle's intellectual prowess.

I nodded. "He liked your play a lot."

"He did?" Malcolm said, perking up. "Elaborate."

"He thought it was funny."

"That's all?" he scowled.

"And smart." Kyle hadn't said that. But I thought it best to appease Malcolm.

He let out another snort. "They tell me his commentary was quite probing." Malcolm took a long gulp of coffee. "But what could a bunch of cops possibly know? Monosyllabic clods."

"Don't they teach Shakespeare at the police academy?"

"Ha, ha," he said. "No wonder you never gave it back. I thought you were hoarding it for the sheer wonder of my genius." He took a sip and winced. "They make the most vile brew here."

"Did they give it back to you?"

"They wouldn't even show me." He lit another cigarette.

"Evidence. Can you imagine? Malcolm Foxman, a cog in the wheels of justice."

"What else did they tell you?"

Malcolm shook his head. "Nothing." He took a long drag on his cigarette. "Except that my masterpiece was used for scrap paper."

"I heard."

"Oh, they told you?" he sighed. "And I thought I was privy to classified information." He stubbed out his cigarette. "Evidently, somebody jotted a message on the first act."

"What an insult."

"At least you understand," Malcolm said. "It wasn't you, was it?"

I gave him a hurt look. "Of course not."

"It couldn't have been," he said. "Unless you know Swedish."

"You've got me there."

"I knew you weren't *that* sophisticated."

"Gee, thanks," I said.

"They wouldn't tell me what it said." Malcolm stirred his coffee thoughtfully. "Just that it was confidential."

"'Confidential,'" I repeated. At least Jacob had been consistent. It was obvious to me now. Christian had jotted a note on the play, probably when he was on his cell phone. I recalled that he'd disappeared into Carmi's bedroom blabbing in his pigeon Arabic. I was certain that's where I'd last seen the play. Then Christian must've walked off with it, the sneaky bastard. That's how it'd ended up in his apartment. And if that was true—which I thought it was—Kyle's story about reading and scribbling on it made sense, too. Maybe Kyle *was* telling the truth.

"What did the cops want with you?" I said.

"They wanted to know if I knew your beast and your Nazi."

"And?" I said.

"What do you mean 'and'?" Malcolm said. "I met them on two separate occasions. You know that."

I did know. But I thought Malcolm might tell me something new.

"And get this," Malcolm said. "They wanted to know my alibi!"

It should've struck me as absurd. But it didn't. It worried me. Was Malcolm a suspect?

"I told them I was grappling with my muse, not a fair-haired Nazi." Malcolm laughed at himself. "It took them forever to figure out what I meant. They probably thought 'muse' was someone's name. Of course," Malcolm continued, "they were jumping to conclusions. I've had my share of run-ins with the law . . ." He winked like I should find this revelation amusing. I didn't.

"What sort of run-ins?" I said.

"Oh, you know," he said, with a shrug. "Mostly, infantile . . ."

"Like what," I said. "Ripping off a Mars bar at your local five-and-dime?"

Malcolm frowned. "You should know me better than that."

That was the problem. I didn't know anyone anymore. Maybe I never had. "Then what?" I said.

He sighed. "If you really must know," he said, wiping his nose with a ratty tissue, "I had a little substance abuse *issue*. Nothing major I assure you."

It was hard to imagine Malcolm with any little issues. I considered pressing him for details about his pesky addiction, but he wasn't paying attention. He was looking around the diner.

"Malcolm," I said. His eyes roamed back to me. "What happened?"

"Oh, nothing much," he said, lighting a cigarette. "Merely a slap on the wrist and a stint in some Betty Ford dump . . . but I'm alright now—as you can see."

I wasn't sure I could see, but I nodded just the same. Now I was certain I hardly knew Malcolm. I was also certain he was a suspect.

Malcolm looked at his watch. "This must be my last," he said, waving around his cigarette. "Then it's back to the coal mines." He flipped over the check and laid out a twenty. "Lunch is on me," he said. "I'm about to be wealthy."

_____PART III

chapter 29

I was waiting for Jan on the corner of 58th and Fifth. He'd called at around four and invited me to meet him. We were going to take a long walk—the day was unseasonably warm—then have dinner. I stood in a patch of fading sun, watching the horse-drawn carriages come and go to my left, the smell of manure in the air. The Plaza Hotel sprawled in front of me like a fairy-tale castle. Screeching brakes and honking horns grated on my nerves. Jacob's advice about staying away from Kyle still bothered me. I couldn't stop thinking about it. What trouble could Kyle cause with two broken arms?

I saw Jan walking toward me, his quick stride so familiar now. He had on a charcoal flannel suit with a white shirt. He wasn't wearing a tie. I found myself admiring him, like the first time I'd seen him; his good looks were still something to marvel at. When he caught sight of me, he waved.

"Sorry I'm late," he said, as he approached me.

"You're hardly late," I said.

He kissed me. "Are you hungry?"

"Not really."

"Do you want to walk?" he said.

"It's a beautiful day."

"Yes," he said. "It was a dumb question."

We headed down a sloped path that wrapped around a sprawling pond. It was a pretty spot even though the water was murky green and smelled of algae. A lone duck broke the mirrored surface, dipping in and out of the water, shaking its dappled feathers.

Jan walked like he had to be somewhere. I had to take two steps to his one. "What's the hurry?" I said.

"Sorry," Jan said. "I'm so used to being on my own."

"And I'm used to my snail's pace."

Jan laughed. We fell into an easy stroll, his muted voice filling my ears with a day's woth of Diamond District adventures. The sky faded into a dusty gray; it was sort of romantic. I thought about telling Jan that I loved him. But I didn't have the nerve. We'd never said it, and I didn't want to be first.

He guided me toward another path that plunged deeper into the park. The rambling trees and miniature rolling hills seemed to go on forever. Soon enough, I could barely hear the traffic tearing down Fifth Avenue. You could get lost if you weren't careful. The thought alarmed me slightly. If I'd been alone, I probably would've made up all kinds of creepy scenarios.

"You know where you're going, right?" I said.

"I have an excellent sense of direction," Jan said, smiling. "I would never get you lost."

"You must come here a lot."

"It helps me think," he said.

"It's so quiet."

"One of the few places," he said, "where you can escape."

Jan paused in front of a bench. He lit a cigarette and smoked thoughtfully; something was on his mind. I hoped it was good. I'd had enough bad news for a few years.

I sat on the edge of the bench and waited, wrapping my scarf around my neck. The day had suddenly gone cold.

Jan didn't sit down. He was standing in front of me, looking up at the canopy of bare trees. He was so tall, his thighs were in my face.

"Sit down," I said.

"I'm fine," he said. "I've been sitting all day."

He examined the trees. "These are probably over one hundred years old."

I looked up, too. "How can you tell?"

"You just can."

"Can you imagine," I said, "that something could live that long in this city?"

"It's amazing," he said, still studying the bare branches. "But I guess they're used to the stress."

If only I could hold up so well.

Jan sat next to me, his leg pressing against mine. I could feel his warmth through the wool of my pants.

"You know," Jan said, looking at the ground, "I've got to leave soon."

So there it was. I'd expected to hear this eventually, of course, though I hadn't exactly spent a lot of time thinking about it. I'd been living in the moment, and now the future was suddenly here. Jan's imminent departure made me realize that I'd have to leave soon, too. I hadn't made any plans, I hadn't packed. I realized I only had a few days left in New York myself.

"Sooner than I thought," he said. "Unfortunately."

"Sooner when?"

Jan threw down his butt and crushed it with the toe of his shoe. "The day after tomorrow."

"The day after *tomorrow*," I repeated. Why had he waited so long to tell me?

He seemed to read my mind. "I didn't want to mention it earlier. I didn't want to spoil our last few days together."

It had worked.

"It's abrupt," he said, grimacing like he'd made a mistake. "I hope you're not mad."

"I'm not mad," I said. "Surprised, but not really . . ."

"Let's make the best of it," Jan said, brightly. "What do you want to do?"

"Not sit here," I said. "I'm cold."

the foreigner_____MEG CASTALDO

Jan pulled me close to him and we pressed on. It was just about dark now. We didn't talk for some time. What was there to say?

I could hear the street rising up in the near distance. We were on the periphery of the real world again. "You know," Jan said, "you never answered me."

"About what?"

"About whether or not you're coming with me."

Jan stopped short. We were on a wooden bridge that spanned across another boggy pond. The wind had kicked up; my hair blew across my face. Jan reached out and tried to tame it. He was watching me intently, waiting for his answer. I could go with him, or back to California; practically speaking, those were my only choices. If I didn't go with Jan, I wondered if I'd ever see him again. I had considered leaving with him, but only fleetingly. I'd spent enough time with Jan to think we'd travel well together. Still, it wasn't an easy decision. And if I agreed, it would be hard to renege.

I said I wasn't sure. Jan seemed satisfied for the time being. We hurried back to the street and jumped in a cab. Jan took me to a fancy restaurant, where we drank a bottle of champagne as though we were celebrating the beginning and not the end.

chapter 30

The next morning I got a call from Louis, the doorman: Kyle was downstairs. They'd obviously released him from the hospital. I didn't want to see him. Wasn't that how I'd ended up in this mess in the first place? Louis buzzed two more times. Kyle wasn't to be put off. Both times, I refused to let him up. Louis said not to worry, he'd show him the door. I couldn't help but feel bad about avoiding Kyle. He was my oldest friend. Regardless, it seemed like the right thing to do.

About fifteen minutes later, the phone rang. I thought it'd be Kyle calling from the corner to curse me. It wasn't.

"Hello, dear," Carmi said, cheerfully.

"Hi, Carmi," I said, with genuine relief in my voice. I was glad to talk to someone outside this mess.

"How are things?"

"Okay," I lied.

"Just okay?"

"Fine," I said. "Maybe a little lonely." I didn't know what compelled me to say that.

"The city's like that," he said.

"I guess."

"You haven't made any friends?"

Friends. I guess you could call Christian that. But he was dead. "Not really," I said.

"Well," Carmi said, "you're probably better off."

Carmi was right. I would've been better off had I minded my own business.

"How's Puerto Rico?" I said.

"Divine," Carmi said.

"Like Eden, then?"

"Down to the apple." Carmi chuckled.

"Great," I said.

I remembered the package that Christian was supposed to have left for him. "Carmi," I said, "your neighbor Christian still hasn't dropped off anything for you." Talking about Christian in the present tense felt wrong. But I wanted to know what Carmi was expecting. I'd already decided that it couldn't be drugs. Carmi didn't even keep over-the-counter stuff in his medicine cabinet.

"Oh," Carmi said. "Don't worry about that."

"I'm not," I said. "I just wondered . . ."

"People today are so busy," he said. "I don't think Christian is very reliable."

It was hard to be reliable when you were dead.

"I'll tell you all about it when I get back," he continued.

"I can't wait," I said. I tried not to sound overly interested.

"Well, I'll see you in a few days."

"Okay," I said.

"We can talk then."

He didn't know the half of it.

Against my better judgment—and Jacob's advice—I ventured out. Despite my anxiety, or maybe because of it, I was hungry. My appetite had begun to reemerge and there was nothing to eat at Carmi's; I couldn't even remember the last time I'd set foot in a store. I checked the weather by pressing my palm against a window. The glass was a sheet of ice.

As I passed Louis, he signaled with his shank-size hand to stop. I waited while he finished his phone call. He hung up and said: "You ought to be more choosy."

I nodded slowly. What else was new.

"That guy. With the broke arm." He bent his own at the elbow to remind me of who we were talking about.

"I know who you mean," I said.

"He's not right in the head."

"You think?" I said, wondering why I was soliciting the opinion of someone called "Louis the China Man."

"Yeah," he said, giving the cuffs of his uniform a yank. "I seen guys like that in the army."

In the army.

"They get so scared . . ." He dodged something imaginary. "You know," he said. "From the bullets." He pointed to his shiny bald head. "Their brains turn *mooshad.*"

Mooshad. It was some bastardized Italian slang for "mush." I'd heard it before from my grandparents. It meant your brains were polenta.

"Thanks," I said, backing away, "for getting rid of him."

"Don't you worry about nothin'," he said, slapping his huge paws together.

"I won't," I said.

"I got a lot of friends." He smiled, his eyes lost in his fleshy red face.

"See ya, Louis," I said.

"You let me know," he said.

It was nice to know I could have Kyle thrown into the East River in cement shoes.

Outside it was clear and frigid; I could see my breath. I scooted down the street, hands deep in my pockets, palms sweating. I passed an alley, the stench reminding me of Yassi— fittingly, I picked up my pace.

I was about to step into the market when Kyle stopped me in my tracks. He must've been waiting all morning for me. His face was wind-blown. Most of his bruises had healed, though he still had a row of stitches above his right eye. He looked a little like Frankenstein. One of his arms was out of the cast.

"I'm not supposed to be seen with you," I said, trying to step around him.

"*What?*" Kyle screwed up his face like he didn't understand a word I was saying.

"We're not supposed to talk."

"Why not?"

"Guilt by association or something," I said. I didn't want to get into particulars with him.

"Are you serious?" Kyle said, like it was the silliest thing he'd ever heard.

"Yes," I said. "Now let me grocery shop."

"I need to talk to you," he said, looking around. "Forget the goddamn bologna."

I don't know why he thought I was buying bologna. I hated bologna. It was sort of funny. I laughed. Maybe that was his strategy.

"I want to talk to you," he repeated.

"I told you," I said, Jacob's advice running in my head like a ticker tape. "I'm not supposed to."

"That's *bullshit,*" he roared.

He was as predictable as ever.

"Who said?" Kyle demanded.

"Never mind," I said.

"Yassi?"

"No."

"Then who?"

"Forget it," I said.

"Forget it? I've known you for eleven years and you say forget it."

I wished he wouldn't pull the guilt thing on me. I wanted to walk away and leave Kyle standing there on the sidewalk with his busted arm. I took a step.

"Wait," he said, reaching out for my shoulder.

"Don't."

"Okay," he said, backing away. "I just want to talk."

"Then talk."

"It's too cold."

"It's not so bad," I said, even though my teeth were chattering.

"My balls are freezing," he said.

"I don't care."

"Let's go in there." He nodded toward a pool hall across the street. The facade was all windows; I could see a pod of pool sharks hovering over billiard tables. It seemed pretty safe, as crazy as that sounded. "Five minutes," I said.

"Whatever you say," Kyle said. I followed him into the hall. There were about thirty tables lined up in three rows with just enough room in between to play. The crowd—mostly young Asian guys— was surprisingly quiet. I guess eight ball required concentration. The air was thick with cigarette smoke. The heat was blasting; I could feel hot gusts coming down on my head. I began peeling off layers even though I knew it'd take me forever to bundle up again.

Kyle took off his flimsy jacket. He'd never really had it on— he'd draped it over his bad arm like a tablecloth. "It fuckin' stinks in here," he said, wrinkling up his nose.

"This was your idea," I said.

"You wouldn't let me come up," he complained.

I didn't bother explaining myself.

We were still standing by the door. A bald guy asked if we wanted a table. Kyle said we did, even though I wasn't in the mood for games. Kyle took our gear to a corner in the back. A dim fluorescent light hung over the faded green baize.

"I used to play for money," Kyle said, as he racked up the balls like a champ. "When I was broke."

I didn't say anything. Did he really think we were going to play?

"You break," he said, rubbing the end of his cue with a cube of blue chalk.

"I don't want to play," I said.

Kyle looked surprised.

"I'll let you win," he said with a grin.

"I don't want to win."

"Everybody wants to fuckin' win," he grumbled.

"Anyway," I said, "how can you play like that?"

Kyle looked down at his bandaged arm. "I'll figure somethin' out."

He leaned over the table. He tried different poses, balancing the cue with his good arm, laying his bad one on the felt. "I guess I can manage," he said.

I started putting on my jacket.

"Hey," he said. "Where you goin'?"

I'd had enough of Kyle's tiptoeing around whatever it was he wanted to talk about. "I shouldn't have listened to you in the first place."

"Will you hold on?" Kyle said. I watched him break. It was pretty lame, the balls clustered in one spot. "Fuck," he said. I didn't make a move to get up. "Your turn."

I'd stay for two more minutes. I yanked the cue from his good hand and took a wild shot at the three ball. It bounced against the bumpers of a corner pocket, but didn't drop. Usually, I was decent. We'd had a table growing up. Years ago, Kyle and I had played a lot. I tried to obliterate the memory.

"Good try," Kyle said, crouching by the table to line up a shot. He paused to look at me. "I wanted to talk to you . . ." he said, lowering his voice, "'cause I missed you."

Sentimentality was so unlike Kyle. I wondered what he was

after now. Or maybe he was playing on my sympathy. "I'm right here," I said.

He examined the line between cue ball and ten. "You know how I got jumped by Cubans?"

"Yeah."

"Well . . . it's not exactly true."

What a surprise. I folded my arms and waited for him to continue.

"I mean . . . they coulda been Cuban." Kyle fired off a shot: the cue ball bounced off the table.

"Damn," he mumbled.

"But they weren't," I said, picking up the ball.

"No," he said.

"Then who were they?" I said, lining up another shot and sawing the cue between thumb and first finger.

"Bad people."

"'Bad people'?" I repeated. Was this a fairy tale? I was still leaning over the table. I turned my head to look at Kyle.

"It's all Yassi's fault," he said, scowling.

"That you got beat up?"

He nodded. I went back to my shot. I knew I'd miss even before I hit the cue ball.

"Your turn," I said.

Kyle didn't move. "I think I'm in trouble."

It was the first time Kyle had ever admitted being in trouble. "With these people?"

"They're gonna come after me again," he said, glancing around like the bad people might be here in the pool hall. He was making me nervous.

"What did you do?" I said.

"Nothin'," he said. "At least I don't think . . ."

"Well you better think," I said. I pulled a stool over and sat down.

Kyle shuffled up close to me. He sucked in a deep breath and told his latest story.

There weren't any Cubans—like he'd already said. Kyle had been hassled by some of Yassi's "friends." At least, that's who he thought they were. He couldn't be sure since they'd hauled off and stomped him before he could get a word in edgewise. They kept asking him for the play. They could only mean Malcolm's manuscript, but he'd given that back to Christian before he died. He'd tried to explain but they didn't buy it. Kyle—in usual dramatic fashion—swore they were going to kill him. This time around it was hard not to believe him.

"It's nice of you to start telling the truth now," I said.

"Yeah, well," Kyle said. "It's complicated."

"Did you tell Jacob this story?"

"The cop?"

I nodded.

"Fuck no," he said. "I don't need those goons all over me again."

"Maybe if you'd stop lying for a change."

"I didn't lie," Kyle said. "I just didn't say anything."

There wasn't much difference between the two.

"What are you going to do?" I said.

Kyle shrugged and leaned against the table. "Maybe go to Philly for a while," he said, thoughtfully.

"Philly."

"Yeah," he said.

I had no idea what awaited Kyle in Philly. But I didn't bother asking. He'd fabricate some story.

"I'm leaving, too." I said.

He perked up. "When?"

"When my uncle gets back," I said. "In a few days."

"Were you even gonna tell me?"

I didn't answer him. I wasn't sure how I felt about Kyle—or how much I should even be telling him. It was just that we'd known each other so long. It was hard to censure myself.

"Are you going back to California?"

"I'm not sure," I said. Lately I'd been leaning more toward traveling for a few weeks with Jan. California would always be there. "I might travel for a while."

"Where?" Kyle said, dropping his cue on the table. He'd given up on playing.

"I'm not sure yet," I said.

"By yourself?"

"With Jan."

"With Jan?" Kyle said. "You can't."

Did Kyle think he was my dad? I could do whatever I wanted. He was just jealous.

"Of course, I can," I said, starting to layer my clothes again. I wanted to leave before this went any further.

"You don't even know that guy," Kyle said, moving in on my space.

"Yes, I do," I said, annoyed at myself for even bothering to defend my position.

"Yeah?" Kyle said. "Well, let me tell you somethin' about your Prince Charming . . ."

"I don't want to hear it," I said, pulling my beret over my ears.

"Wait a sec," Kyle said, positioning himself so close to me that I'd have to shove him to get by. "Just hear me out . . ."

I sighed. I was sweating already. I hated the furnacelike quality of New York's indoor spaces more than I hated the cold. I closed my eyes for a minute; I was losing patience. Kyle—I knew from years of experience—wouldn't give up until he'd unloaded on me.

"Remember that night in the bar?" he continued. "You felt

shitty, so you split?" I could still picture Kyle and Jan hovering over the table, empty shot glasses between them. "Well, that's when Jan and I really started to suck up some booze . . . we had, like, two more rounds of whisky. Then—don't get mad . . ." he said, staring at me sheepishly, "I wanted to call Christian and score. I didn't have any coin so I asked Jan to come with me and pay for it. But Jan said he wasn't into smoking dope because it made him edgy or some shit."

As far as I knew, Jan wasn't interested in drugs. I wasn't either. I never really had been—ever since I'd passed out in a cafe in Amsterdam and ended up at the other end of town without knowing how I actually got there . . . but that was a long time ago.

"Jan started askin' me all kinds of shit about Christian," he said, "like if I knew how much you'd seen him and stuff."

Kyle seemed to be making this part up. I didn't doubt that Kyle had asked Jan to buy dope for him. Kyle would ask anyone even remotely in his orbit. But I couldn't see why Jan would have any interest in Christian. "What did you tell him?" I said.

"I told Jan that Christian bought you shoes."

I jumped off the stool. "You did?"

"Yeah," Kyle said triumphantly. "So what?"

"You're a bastard," I said, wishing I'd never told Kyle. Any bit of information became his ammunition.

Kyle ignored me. He was just warming up now. "So he got all freaked out and started askin' a lot more questions."

"Shut up," I said. He was beginning to make me sick.

"I'm not finished," Kyle said, snarling. "It got pretty ugly when I told Jan that Christian was always tryin' to do you . . ."

"You're lying," I said. His tone was beginning to take on that unreal quality, that drug-induced blabbermouth syndrome that I'd come to know all too well. "Conversation over," I said, pushing past him and heading toward the door. He followed my heels, his gravelly voice still audible.

"I'm not lying," he continued. "He said he was gonna go over to Christian's and beat the fuck out of him . . . I swear."

I was already on the street, heading back to Carmi's. Louis the doorman would make sure Kyle didn't get past the lobby. One more block of listening to his crap. I cursed the light for turning red.

Kyle lumbered up next to me. His face was serious for a change. "Alex," he said, "whatever you do, don't go anywhere with him." He let his good hand gently rest on top of my head. I didn't shake him off. Nostalgia kicking in one last time. "I don't fuckin' trust him . . . I'm only saying it 'cause I love you."

He was only saying it because he didn't want me to leave him. The light turned green. I gave him one look—maybe my last—and left him standing on the corner, yelling my name. I sprinted back to Carmi's, panting like a racehorse. I wouldn't have been surprised if someone told me I was foaming at the mouth. I blew past Louis without even seeing him. He stopped me to say that "some lady with a bald head—almost as bald as my own—was lookin' for you." It didn't even phase me. I told Louis he wasn't to let her up under any circumstances. In fact, he could call the cops or one of his so-called friends for all I cared.

chapter 31

I didn't spend too much time brooding over what Kyle said. I ordered in a pizza and chomped down two slices—even though they were cold and soggy—thinking that, at the very least, Kyle hadn't managed to ruin my appetite. I knew that he'd probably told Jan about the shoes. But Jan had never brought it up. He was too much of a gentleman. All the other stuff was outlandish.

I was just sticking the rest of the pizza in the fridge when the phone rang. It was Jan; he was at a pay phone. I could barely hear him over the background noise.

"Alex," he said.

"Hi," I said, recognizing his voice.

"I want to see you."

"Where are you?" I said, competing with a blaring horn.

"What?"

"Where are you?" I repeated.

"Close by," he said. "Can you come down?"

"Now?"

"Yes," he said, excitedly. "I have a surprise for you."

"What kind of surprise?"

"I don't want to tell you," he said, chuckling. "Then it won't be a surprise."

"Okay," I said. "Why don't you come up?"

"No," he said. "You come down."

"Where are you?"

"Just come down," he said. "I'll be in the lobby."

I didn't feel like venturing out into the cold again. But Jan's good mood was almost contagious.

"Alright," I said. "I'll see you in a few minutes."

"Okay," he said, hanging up the phone.

This was our last night together. I could tell. That's why he hadn't wanted to come up. He must have planned something different—I liked the idea. While I quickly brushed my teeth, I thought about what I'd tell him. I'd have to give him my answer. There was nothing actually keeping me from going. Carmi would be back in three days. The apartment would only be empty for two. I'd call my parents in the morning. They'd think I was crazy; but I was twenty-eight—old enough to do what I wanted. They knew about Jan, and they trusted me. Besides, I didn't want to give Jan up so soon. Prolonging our inevitable parting wouldn't be the worst thing in the world. I'd be back in California in less than a month. Meanwhile, I'd spend a couple of weeks in Belgium. Maybe we'd go to Paris. Then I'd come back. What did I have to lose?

When I stepped into the corridor, a small group was milling around with the super. He gave me a look that said *Don't say a word.* Maybe he had a scam going—visit an actual murder site for ten bucks. It made me queasy. Then it hit me: They were here to rent Christian's apartment. They didn't know that someone had been killed in there—or they didn't care. I suppose the super had already whitewashed the blood on the wall and upped the rent by five hundred bucks.

Jan was in the lobby. He looked as though he'd walked thirty blocks in the wind. His hair was tousled; his face rosy. He was all smiles. I was happy to see him, too. He told me we were spending the night in a posh hotel on the Upper East Side—that was his surprise. The fact that he'd made a romantic plan only made him more attractive. I'd never been to his last hotel—I'd only been in the lobby, where I'd met his client Eddie. Jan hadn't wanted to take me there; he said his room wasn't much to look at. It was cramped and noisy. That was okay with me. In the beginning, I'd wanted to be on my own turf.

The hotel was one of those over-the-top numbers that old rich people with tiny yappy dogs stay in. The lobby was decked out in white marble with black swirls, gigantic floral arrangements studded with stargazer lilies and an army-size staff in burgundy uniforms with gold braided trim. While Jan checked in, I stood in front of the elevator watching well-dressed people come and go. A bellhop asked me if I had any luggage. It was fun telling him no. He probably thought I was a call girl.

Jan had his little black suitcase in his hand. He had dropped it off earlier. "Well," he said, as we stepped into the elevator. "What do you think?"

"Fancy."

"I thought it might be fun to pretend that we're rich."

"You are," I said. "Aren't you?"

"I have my resources," he said, smiling.

Jan obviously had money. It hadn't occurred to me before.

The room was large with a king-size bed, ornate rosewood-colored furniture, brass lamps, and thick swags of drapery. It was so stuffy-looking that we both laughed. "It isn't quite what I expected," Jan said, glancing around.

"It's perfect," I said. It suited Jan in a way. It had Old World charm.

"Are you sure?"

"Of course," I said, heading into the bathroom and flipping on the light. It was the size of Carmi's living room. "This is great."

Jan mixed drinks from the minibar. I sat on the bed and watched him. He handed me a gin and tonic and sunk into the love seat against the wall. I sipped my cocktail; it sent a chill down my spine.

"You leave tomorrow," I said. I wanted to get it out in the open.

Jan nodded and took a long sip. "I have to get back."

"I understand," I said, taking another gulp of my gin. I needed courage to tell him that I wanted to go.

"So?"

"So," I said.

"Are you coming?"

"Are you sure you want me to?"

Jan placed his drink on the desk. He sat on the bed next to me and gave me a long kiss. "I want you to come with me," he said. "You can stay two days or two weeks. It's up to you . . ."

"Alright," I said. "Then let's go."

He smiled. "Then it's settled."

"Deal," I said, chugging the rest of my cocktail. I wanted to celebrate, but something was making me feel apprehensive. Maybe it was what Kyle had said—though I didn't believe him. Or maybe it was because I'd never done anything like this before.

Jan was rooting around in his suitcase. "I was saving this for later," he said, handing me a pink silk pouch. "But I can't wait."

I held the pouch in my hands. I didn't want to rush opening it. I smiled at the thought of him picking something out for me. It'd been a long time since I received anything nice from a man— with the exception of the shoes, of course. And I hadn't wanted those in the first place.

"Open it," he said.

I stretched the black cord and turned the contents over in my palm. A gold chain dotted with tiny diamonds. It was beautiful.

"It belonged to an Indian woman," Jan said. "It's pretty old."

"It's beautiful," I said, admiring it. I recalled the Indian legend about diamonds warding off danger; I wondered if Jan knew the lore. Then it dawned on me: "I don't have anything for you," I said, feeling like a fool.

"I don't want anything," he said, putting the necklace around my neck. "Go look."

I hurried into the palatial bathroom. The necklace rested in the cuplike indentation at the center of my collarbone—it was the perfect length. My olive skin showed through the filigree. If it weren't for the diamonds, it could've been a henna tattoo. It was absolutely right. I yelled to Jan in the other room.

"I'm glad," he said.

I came out of the bathroom.

"Wear it once in a while," he said. "And think of me . . ."

"I'll wear it all the time," I said. I wouldn't need a necklace to think about him. That had become automatic.

chapter 32

We went out to dinner late. I had a pounding headache from the three rounds of gin and Jan was antsy. He wanted a break from the "Sun King's hangout"—that's what he called our room. We braved the icy night and took a cab to a cramped Indian restaurant in the Village. The place was done up with hundreds of blinking chili pepper lights strung across the windows. The walls were covered in children's dress fabric dotted with words: *blue, cat, crayon,* and so on. The ceiling was completely hidden beneath paper decorations—the kind you get from the drug store. The tiny rectangular room looked like a parade float. I wouldn't have been surprised if the place moved—propelled by chaos alone. It was crowded, even though it was well after ten.

We snagged a table in the back near the clamoring kitchen, the Indian pop music competing with the sea of voices. A waiter, who looked about sixteen, came by. Jan ordered beer.

"How did you ever find this place?" I said, leaning across the tiny table.

"Don't you like it?" he said, smiling.

"I love it," I said, glancing around.

"It reminds me," Jan said, "of the real thing."

"India, you mean."

Jan nodded. "The smell more than anything."

The air was so choked with cooking odors, I could feel them seeping into my hair and clothes.

It occurred to me that I didn't know the particulars about tomorrow. "What time are we leaving?" I asked.

"Late," he said, pausing from the menu. "Around eight. You'll have all day to get ready."

I nodded. Tomorrow was a long way off. It still didn't seem real.

"Will you call your parents?" he asked.

It was an odd question. I figured he was just being polite. "Of course," I said.

"What will you tell them?"

"That I'm going to Europe with you."

He nodded. The waiter stopped by again. Jan ordered for us. I wasn't all that familiar with Indian food so that was okay with me. Then he settled back in his chair. "What about your uncle?" he asked.

"I'll leave him a note," I said.

"You'll tell him the same thing?"

"Yes," I said. "Stop worrying. I'll take care of everything."

He nodded. "Good," he said, breaking off a piece of poppadum. "What about Kyle?" he said.

"Don't remind me," I said, picturing his face.

"Will you tell him?"

"I already did."

Jan leaned over the table, his eyes wide. "When did you see him?"

"Today," I said.

"I thought you weren't speaking." Jan seemed slightly annoyed.

"We're not," I said. "At least I'm not supposed to . . ."

"What did he want?" Jan said.

"To talk," I said, recalling our conversation—though you could barely call it that.

"What did he have to say for himself?"

"A bunch of crap," I said, scooting in my chair. I kept getting bumped by waiters balancing platters of sizzling shrimp, puffy balls of bread, and tiny silver dishes piled with things that I didn't recognize.

"What kind of crap?"

"About Christian," I said. "And if you really must know, about you . . ." Just thinking about Kyle's stupid story made me irate.

"About me?" Jan said, his voice breaking its usual even tone. "What could he possibly say about me?"

"Never mind," I said, wishing I hadn't opened my big mouth. It was the damn beer.

"No," he said, reaching across the table and grabbing my hand. "Tell me everything."

"It's really just a bunch of shit—Kyle shit—it'll only piss you off . . ."

"Alex," he said, squeezing me fingers. "I want to know."

"Alright, alright," I said. He was being as persistent as Kyle. What did it matter if he hated Kyle? He'd never see him again. "Kyle said you went over to Christian's that night . . . because you were angry . . ."

"What night?'"

"The night Christian got killed," I said.

"That's ridiculous," Jan said, scowling. "I didn't even know him. Besides, I dropped by Eddie's hotel to say good-bye to him before I came to see you."

"You don't have to defend yourself," I said. "Calm down."

"I am calm," he said. "But he's lying."

The waiter interrupted us, dropping off about eight different dishes of various colors and textures. We tucked in. I was suddenly ravenous. It had been a long time since the mushy pizza. Jan must've felt the same way because we hardly said a word until half the plates were empty.

"I didn't want to have to tell you this," Jan said, finishing his beer.

"Tell me what?"

Jan shook his head and sighed, like he still hadn't made up his mind.

"Say what?" I repeated, tearing off a piece of bread.

"I've been thinking about what you said."

the foreigner_____MEG CASTALDO

"About Kyle?"

"About the night in the bar," Jan said, pushing his plate away from him. "The night Christian was killed."

Whatever he was about to say wasn't going to be good.

"You've already told Jacob everything," I said.

"Not quite everything," Jan said. A busboy noisily picked up our dishes. He followed up with tea and mango ice cream "from the house."

"Oh, Christ," I said. I felt the blood draining from my face.

Jan raised his thick eyebrows.

"It's about Kyle," I said. It was obvious.

Jan nodded. "I left a few things out of my statement," he said. "Because I thought it was nothing."

I was beginning to catch on. Jan had lied for Kyle—on my account. I wasn't sure how that made me feel.

"Don't get me wrong," he continued. "I like Kyle, as much as anyone can actually like Kyle." He smiled. "He's amusing."

Amusing wasn't the first thing that came to mind.

"And I know he's a very old friend."

"If he's involved in this—" I said.

"I think he was," Jan said, cutting me off. "And still is . . ."

I felt like I'd just skipped ahead to the end of a mystery.

"I wasn't going to say anything," Jan said. "But after what he told you . . ."

I nodded. It was all becoming clear.

"So do you want to hear this?" he said.

"Do I have a choice?"

He laughed. "No."

"Then go ahead," I said. I worked on polishing off the ice cream while Jan talked.

"After you left us in the bar, we had another round of whisky. We were actually having an okay time." He took a sip of tea. "We talked about New York, Europe. He tried out his French on me." I didn't know Kyle had any French to try. "It was pretty dismal," Jan continued, smiling. "Kyle wanted to continue drinking." No surprise there either. "But I had to leave. I had to stop by Eddie's hotel. And I wanted to get back to you." Jan scooped up the last bit of ice cream. "Kyle wanted to know if I'd ever bought any dope from Christian. Of course, I said no. Kyle said he was going to call him, that Christian owed him."

"Owed him for what?"

"Drugs, I guess," he shrugged. "So it's very possible that Kyle went to see Christian that night."

"It's possible," I said, blowing on my tea. "But it doesn't mean he killed him."

"He said one thing that's been nagging me all along," Jan said.

"There's more?"

"Yes," Jan said. "Kyle told me he'd paid Christian and Christian never delivered . . . Kyle wanted to scare Christian."

"You mean threaten him."

"That's what I mean."

"You think," I said, following his logic, "that Kyle bashed Christian's head against the wall because he owed him some dope?"

"Someone pushed him," Jan said. "Someone strong."

Kyle was strong . . . "But Kyle wouldn't kill anyone."

"He might not have meant to," Jan said.

I heard myself repeat: *He might not have meant to.* Of course, I didn't think that Kyle was a killer—but he could easily kill some one accidentally.

"Kyle told me he'd hurt Christian," Jan said, "if he didn't give him what he wanted."

"That's what he told you?" I said.

"Those were his exact words."

I felt almost as sick as I had when I'd found Christian in his bedroom. I was sweating all over and cold. "I don't believe it," I whispered. But it was adding up, what Jacob had said, what Kyle had said himself—he'd admitted to buying from Christian—and now what Jan was saying . . . how much more evidence did I need?

The waiter brought the check. People were still lining up for tables. They probably wanted to get rid of us.

"What are you going to do?" I said, hesitantly.

"I'm going to call Jacob," Jan said, finishing his tea and taking out his wallet, "as soon as we get back to the hotel."

Then it was over. They'd arrest him.

We didn't say anything for a while. I rehashed our conversation in my head; Jan absently stroked my hand while he waited for his change. I was trying to come up with excuses for Kyle—reasons why he wouldn't have bashed Christian's skull into a wall. I was convinced Kyle would never hurt anyone intentionally. But crimes of passion happened all the time—they were still crimes. I knew Kyle wasn't the sort of man who went through life restraining himself.

"I still can't believe he did it," I said, though my tone sounded like someone who was already convinced.

I thought I would've slept well in a hotel bed with plush sheets and Jan next to me. But I didn't. Maybe I had Kyle on my mind; maybe I was nervous about going back to Europe with Jan. Whatever the reason, I woke with a start. I felt like I was suffocating. Jan was sitting at the desk. In the soft gray light, it was hard to make out what he was doing. He was on the phone speaking French in a low voice. I couldn't understand what he was saying—only fragments came to me. I had no idea what time it was. I wondered who he was talking to. I tried to rouse myself from the torpor of sleep. But I rolled over and passed out again.

When I came to—about seven—Jan wasn't in the room. I wasn't an early riser but I got up and pulled back the heavy drapes. It was dismal out; the sun hidden behind a smattering of dirty clouds. I slipped into one of the hotel's thick white terry robes with the crest on the pocket; Jan hadn't touched his. It was still hanging on the back of the bathroom door. He'd probably gone out for a French newspaper.

I wandered around the room. Then I snapped on the TV. I always liked watching TV in hotels; it completed the artificial mood. I flipped through the channels until I found the morning news. Then I sat at the desk and ordered room service. I had to move Jan's mess of papers to find the menu. I noticed that he had two passports, which struck me as odd. One from Belgium— predictably—and the other from Suriname. I wondered what tie he had to South America. He also had a lot of money—stacks of it. I figured the gem business was mostly cash. Still, I had the feeling I had a lot to learn about Jan.

He returned with two cappuccinos and a pile of newspapers. While we sipped coffee, we mapped out the day. I'd take a cab to Carmi's and ready the place for his return. Then I'd pack and call my mother. Jan would pick me up around five and we'd be on our way.

chapter 33

I asked the cab driver to let me off about ten blocks from Carmi's apartment so I could walk through Manhattan one last time. I was just beginning to wallow in my New York regret when I stepped into Carmi's lobby and ran smack into Jacob. He was impatiently milling about, like he'd been waiting a while. When he saw me, he gave me a half smile.

"What a surprise," I said.

"Cute," he said.

I wasn't trying to be cute. I'd only wanted to lighten the mood. It had backfired.

"Louis told me you weren't home," he said, sizing me up. I wondered if he was going to ask me where I'd been.

"What can I do for you now," I said wearily.

Jacob looked around. "Let's take a walk," he said, nodding toward the door.

"Do I have to?" I said, unzipping my coat. "I just walked ten blocks."

"Suit yourself," he said, motioning toward a wooden bench near the mailboxes. We sat down. I was closer to Jacob than I wanted to be but the bench was short. I couldn't help but notice that he smelled especially nice—not like cologne—just clean.

"Van den Hoven called me," he said. "He filled me in on a few more details about your friend, Hangerman."

It was weird hearing Jan referred to by his last name. My heart was beating louder and quicker than usual. "Kyle," I said, like I was pronouncing a foreign word.

"We had him picked up."

"So he did it . . . ," I said, my voice barely audible.

"Looks that way," Jacob said. "He's got some crazy alibi we're checking."

"Then maybe . . ."

"It sounds like a crock," Jacob said, shaking his head.

He was sure. I could tell.

"Don't take it so hard," he said, giving me a quick glance.

I didn't offer anything. Hearing it from Jan had been one thing. This was something else.

Jacob stood up. He wasn't very tall. "One more thing," he said.

"What?"

"I'm probably gonna need you to testify."

"Against Kyle . . ."

"No," he said, winking. "Against me."

With that, he turned abruptly on his heel. "I'll call you," he said, as he headed to the door. I stood there for a moment inhaling the scent Jacob had left behind.

Louis emerged from his secret doorman hideout. "Did that frigging pill—excuse the language—finally leave?"

"He's gone, Louis," I said, as I trudged toward the elevator.

"Thank, God," he said, kissing his hand and turning his eyes toward heaven. "That guy makes me nervous. He's always moving. You notice?"

"Yeah, Louis," I said, "I noticed." The elevator doors started to close. "See ya, Louis," I said.

On the way up, I imagined Kyle being dragged away in chains. I thought I'd feel worse, but all I felt was relieved.

I spent most of the day cleaning Carmi's place. I wanted him to find it immaculate. I called my mother. Surprisingly, she thought it'd be a good idea if I took a vacation, especially after all that had happened. She even offered to wire me money, which I took her up on. I didn't tell her that I was actually going to spend the entire trip with Jan. That was too unseemly for my parents. Instead, I said that he'd been visiting New York, and we'd leave for Europe together. It was all a little too convenient. But my mother seemed satisfied. I told her I'd leave Carmi a note, and she said she'd check in with him as soon as he returned to explain my absence. Otherwise, he'd think I'd been kidnapped. I was to call her when I arrived in Belgium.

I must've wrote five notes to Carmi before I ended up with something that didn't make me sound like a flighty twit. I explained to him that I was taking a trip to Belgium. Just one of those spur-of-the-moment jaunts to another continent. It sounded like a fourth grader who'd decided to spend the night at a friend's house. It also sounded glamorous—the sort of thing I'd always seen myself doing. I could just imagine Carmi sitting down at his desk to read my note, his big eyes growing wider with every word. I wrapped up by saying how happy I'd been in his place. I thanked him profusely. I omitted the bit about the murder next door; the building people would fill him in on that.

I made a trip to the grocery store to replenish Carmi's fridge and shelves. I hit the liquor store for three bottles of top-shelf hard stuff. I even bought a bunch of yellow roses, which I arranged around the apartment. Then I turned my attention to packing, which took all of an hour. I hadn't brought much with me in the first place. When every last thing I could think of was done, I sat on Carmi's couch and let my mind run amuck. I still hadn't accepted the fact that Kyle had been arrested. It just didn't seem real.

The car service was right on time. I slid across the backseat next to Jan. He kissed me a bunch of times and said he was glad I was joining him. I wouldn't be disappointed—he'd make it worth my while. I was excited, too. I felt like I'd made the right choice. The first right one in a very long time. I watched Manhattan passing by as the car rumbled through the congested streets. We flew onto the Long Island Expressway only to end up in a colossal traffic jam.

Jan glanced at his watch. "I hope we won't be late."

"We have plenty of time," I said.

He craned his neck to see the traffic ahead of us. "I think there's an accident," Jan said to himself. He leaned back against the seat. The car inched along.

"This is for you," he said, taking a ticket out of his pocket and handing it to me.

"Thanks," I said, opening it. The confirmation was in my name. But the destination cities had been blacked out. "I don't get it," I said.

"It's an itinerary," he said, smiling.

"I can see that."

"I changed our plans slightly," he said.

I looked at Jan to see if he was joking. "Where are we going?"

"Somewhere warm," he said.

Warm. I had a suitcase full of sweaters and wool pants.

"Why are the cities blacked out?"

"I want to surprise you," Jan said.

That was an understatement. The hotel had been a surprise. The necklace had been a surprise. But this . . . this was just nuts. I told him so.

"Don't be upset," Jan said. "Enjoy it." He was still smiling. I could tell he was having fun.

We started moving again, the car lunging forward like a horse unbridled. "I'm not upset," I said. "Just a little flabbergasted."

"That was the idea."

I didn't quite know what to say. Jan's amusement was palpable. Still, I didn't like handing my fate over to someone—even if that someone was Jan. I was getting cold feet. I'd never acted so impulsively. But how could I turn back now? I inspected the confirmation again. "Why can't you tell me where we're going?"

"I don't want to spoil it."

"You won't," I said. "Just tell me."

"You'll love it," he said. "Trust me."

I did trust him. I told him so.

"Be intrigued," Jan said, cheerfully.

"I *am* intrigued," I said. "But I think I'd rather know."

"But I don't want to tell you," he said. "I know this is crazy," he continued, stroking my cheek. "But don't ruin it . . ."

I didn't want to ruin it for him or for me. I could tell that he'd thought about this plan for a long time. Jan was certainly imaginative. He'd wanted to do something totally different. And he wasn't going to give in. That was obvious to me. So by the time we arrived at the airport, I'd stopped asking. I knew that telling me would mean more than simply revealing where we were going. It would also mean that I didn't trust him. In a way, I felt like Jan was testing me. I couldn't help but wonder if I'd pass.

We had time to kill so we ended up in a cafeteria in the middle of the airport; the same place I'd first spoken to Jacob. Two paper cups of burned coffee sat on the table between us; a TV buzzed above our heads. People lugged overstuffed suitcases and weeping kids. Unrecognizable languages floated in the air. I didn't ask Jan where we were going again. I realized that he couldn't keep his secret forever: I'd know by the time we were at the gate. But why keep up the charade until then? It was illogical. For the first time, I didn't understand Jan.

An announcement cut through the din.

"That's us," Jan said, gathering up his newspaper. The announcer had rattled off five boarding calls. Jan didn't make a move to get up.

"Okay," I said, my stomach doing a back flip.

"One last cigarette," he said, striking a match. I smoked, too. I was such a lightweight that the nicotine went straight to my head; a tingle spread through my limbs. We hadn't said much since we arrived. Jan seemed preoccupied. Maybe he was upset by my lack of enthusiasm for his plan. I couldn't help but feel that I was the cause of his dark mood. I reached across the table and took his hand in mine. His palm was warm and sticky.

"Are you okay?" I said. Jan's hands were never sweaty.

He stubbed out his cigarette after two drags. "Fine," he said.

"You're angry," I said. It was an observation, not a question.

He didn't say anything. I took his silence for a yes. Great, I thought, we're having our first fight on the day we're supposed to leave together. It didn't bode well.

"I'm sorry," I said, not really knowing why I was apologizing. I hated confrontations. I wanted this to blow over.

"I only wish," he said, standing up and looking down at me with his cool blue eyes, "that you'd trust me . . ."

We were back to that again. Why had Jan suddenly turned heavy on me? "I *do*," I said, with as much emphasis as I could muster.

Jan still had his eyes focused on me. "I don't think you do," he said.

I let out a sigh. I could play the accusation game too. "Do you trust *me*?" I said.

Jan didn't answer. He could only mean no. I turned my back to him and maneuvered my way around the tables and out of the restaurant. If Jan was trying to pick a fight with me, he'd succeeded. His timing was terrible.

He caught up with me and we wandered along the concourse toward the departure gates, a wide swath of pink carpet stretched endlessly before us. I began to wonder if I was doing the right thing. I'd been so sure today. Now indecisiveness had struck like a lightening bolt. I glanced sideways at Jan. He was staring straight ahead, walking fast as though he was alone. Maybe he was . . . maybe he wanted to be.

Someone yelled from ten paces behind us. It sounded weirdly like Kyle, but that was impossible. He was in jail—or so I thought. I should've trusted my ears. When I glanced over my shoulder, Kyle was practically on top of us, breathing hard like he'd run through the terminal. He looked like a lunatic. He was unshaven; his hair was dirty. His jacket had a gaping hole in the sleeve and his remaining cast was filthy and tattered. He could've been an escapee from Bellevue. I figured he was out on bail, but what the hell was he doing here? He must have followed me—stalker that he'd recently become.

"Where are you going?" Kyle demanded. He was hardly conscious of Jan.

"Away," I said.

"With *him?*" he said, pointing a long index finger at Jan's chest.

"Don't touch me," Jan said, backing up.

"You lied about me," Kyle said to Jan.

"You lied about *me,*" Jan said, calmly.

So now they were even. Kyle turned his eyes on me. "What the fuck are you doin'?" he said.

"Going away," I said. "I already told you."

"You can't," he said, wrapping his good hand around my wrist and dragging me away from Jan. I struggled to untangle myself. "Stop making a scene," I said. But it only went from bad to worse. Jan gave Kyle a hard shove that sent him backpedaling. He nearly fell over. I thought I was seeing things. Jan didn't seem like the type to get his hands dirty.

"Get lost," Jan said. "She doesn't want to talk to you."

Kyle was trying to decide how to proceed. I'd seen that blank look before, but now he seemed uneasy, too, like he hadn't expected Jan—or me—to put up a fight.

"Alex," Kyle started in again, "this guy's a liar." He gave Jan another hard look.

Jan shook his head like he couldn't believe his bad luck.

There was another announcement.

"I'm going," Jan said to me. "Are you coming or not?" All the excitement had been poached from his voice. He was at the end of his rope with me. I could tell. It was now or never.

I picked up my bag and started walking alongside Jan. I took my ticket out of my coat pocket and handed it to him. Kyle followed on our heels, his voice ringing in my ears. *Don't trust him, Alex . . . you don't even know him . . . he tried to bury me,* and so on. A couple in matching track suits stopped and stared. I was mortified.

Jan didn't even turn around to acknowledge Kyle. He hissed at me: "I can't believe you're still talking to him."

Suddenly, I saw Kyle's hand whiz by my ear. He almost hit me in the head. His fist landed somewhere near Jan's neck. Jan swung around for the last time and pushed Kyle so hard that he practically flew through the airport. I didn't think Jan had it in him. Kyle landed on the floor on his bad arm, balled up, and started cursing at the top of his lungs. People were gawking at us. Jan nodded at them and said everything was fine. I wanted to disappear.

"You think you can fuck me over," Kyle said, leaning on his knees and cradling his arm.

Jan looked at him blankly. "You're pathetic," he said.

"Enough," I said to Jan. I bent down next to Kyle. "Are you okay?" I whispered.

"Do I look okay?" he said.

"Why are you here?" I said again. "You're supposed to be in jail."

"Yeah, well," he said, standing up. "They let me out."

A tide of relief washed over me. But did that mean Kyle was innocent or had someone simply posted bail for him? I realized Kyle looked ill. I touched his forehead with the back of my hand. It was red hot. "I think you have a fever," I said.

"I'm sick," he said.

"Go home."

"Where's that?" he said.

It was a good question.

"California," I said.

I helped Kyle stand up. He weighed a ton. "What about you?" he whispered. "Where are you going?"

"I already told you," I said.

Kyle shook his head. "For once in my life," he said, "I'm actually tellin' you the truth."

"I'll be fine," I said. Though I wasn't so certain.

Kyle pulled me toward him and hugged me tightly. "Whatever," he said, giving up. When I broke away from him, Jan was gone. He'd left my bag sitting on the floor two feet away from me. I abandoned Kyle in the middle of the crowd. He'd shaken me up, made me think twice about what I was doing. If Jan hadn't been so mysterious . . . Could I really do this? I decided I couldn't. But I wanted to say good-bye. I wanted to explain myself. Jan deserved that much.

Up ahead I could see Jan navigating his way through knots of people, taking huge strides. I grabbed my bag and hurried after him. By the time I caught up, he was already in line at the metal detectors. He looked at me distractedly, like he hardly recognized me. "I couldn't stand it any longer," he said.

"That's alright," I said. Neither could I. The moment had come.

He cupped my elbow. "I can't wait to get out of here."

"I know," I said, wondering how I was going to break the news to him.

"I don't think you do," he said.

It was happening too fast. We were at the front of the line now. All I had to do was pass through the metal detector and that would be it. I'd be on my way. Jan was showing our tickets to the guard. Another officer motioned for me to place my bag on the conveyor. I didn't. I stepped out of the way.

"What are you doing?" Jan asked.

"I can't," I said. "I'm sorry."

He face fell into a frown. "Of course," he said, "you can."

I shook my head.

"Is it because of Kyle?" Jan said, like he couldn't believe it. "What he said about me?"

Maybe it was. I couldn't say. All I knew was I couldn't go with Jan, wherever he was headed.

"Does it make any difference to you that I love you?" he said, his eyes roaming over my face.

Strangely, it didn't make a difference. Maybe if he'd told me earlier. Maybe if I didn't feel manipulated, like he was saying it so I'd go.

"I guess," he said, letting out a sigh, "this is the end for us."

"I'm sorry," I said again. It seemed to be the only phrase I was capable of uttering lately.

"I want you to know something," he said, taking my hand and staring into my eyes. "I've done so much for you."

I started to pull away. "What have you done?"

the foreigner_____**MEG CASTALDO**

"I have saved you," he said, ". . . from yourself."

Saved me. Had I been lost?

Jan inspected my face. When I didn't budge, he shook his head, brushed his lips against my cheek and released me. Then he quickly retreated, passing under the metal detector and collecting his suitcase on the other side. Jan hurried down the corridor without so much as looking back. I was stunned and disappointed. Stunned that things had gone sour so fast; disappointed in myself for botching our last few minutes. Whatever we'd shared—not love, but something close—was forever spoiled by my clumsiness. I replayed Jan's line about saving me. What was that all about? I must've stood there for fifteen minutes, my mind repeating *I have saved you from yourself.* I'm still not sure what he meant. Maybe I never will be.

I retraced my steps back to the street. I was too exhausted to notice much except that Kyle was nowhere to be found. Outside, I waited for a cab. When I finally got one, I slouched in the backseat, hardly seeing Queens pass by. I rolled down the window even though it was cold. *I have saved you from yourself.* I remembered my itinerary. I took it out of my pocket and stared at the blackened lines; I tried to imagine Jan's secret destination, but I couldn't. It was a blank—just like Jan was to me now.

The cabby broke the spell. He'd been checking me out in the rearview mirror. He wanted to know if I was from India. I looked at his license; his name was Sajit Chaudurry.

"Yes," I said. "Calcutta."

That was the last I ever saw of Jan Van den Hoven. About a year later, I received a postcard that Carmi had forwarded from New York. You couldn't read the postmark and it didn't have a return address. There was a dancing Vishnu on the front. It said:

Dear Alex,

Often you come into my mind when I'm meditating. I have found a kind of peace. I hope you have, too. I wonder about you. If you've found yourself somewhere, if you're not lost. You're often in my thoughts.

Om Shanti,

Jan

chapter 34

When I got back from the airport, the lights were on in Carmi's apartment. I half-expected to see my uncle back in his favorite chair, showing off his tan and sipping a gimlet. I should've known better. Carmi wasn't one to act impulsively. Instead, I found Jacob the party promoter–detective in the living room. He was reading a newspaper.

"Sorry," he said, jumping up as I walked in. "Didn't mean to frighten you." I was surprised to see him on my turf again, but not by much.

"You always let yourself in?" I said.

"You weren't home." A smiled played on his lips. He noticed my bag. "Going somewhere?"

"I thought I was," I said, flopping on Carmi's easy chair.

"What happened?"

"Changed my mind."

He looked around the room for a minute. "Come from the airport?"

I nodded. I didn't bother with why he needed to ask.

"I've got some news for you."

"I figured."

"You're not gonna like it."

I slouched even more and looked at the ceiling. My mouth was so dry I could barely speak.

"This Jan guy," he said. "How long you know him?"

So now we were talking about Jan. There could only be one reason why.

"About a year, I guess." I was finding it hard to form words.

"You guess?"

"I met him in Europe."

"So you said." Out came the black notebook. He leaned

across the coffee table and showed me a page with Jan's name written on it in small cramped letters. "This how he spells his name?"

I nodded. It was a stupid question.

He started jotting things down. "And?" he said.

"And what?"

He stopped writing and caught my eye. "And what happened—when you met in Europe?"

"Nothing happened. I went to Belgium for a few days."

"European vacation. After you got fired from the ad agency. I know about that."

"How?"

"Jan."

"Then why ask?"

"Other inconsistencies in his statement."

"Oh." Inconsistencies, I thought. In his statement. Which meant his statement was inconsistent.

"So he comes here to see you."

"No," I said. "To work."

"And you just happened to be here."

"Yes," I said. "I still happen to be here." I wished I wasn't.

He paused, pen tapping his notebook.

"Was he in love with you?" Jacob said.

It didn't seem like a standard police question. Next, he'd be asking about our sexual activities. "He said he was." Jan had only said it once, and I wasn't sure I even believed him. But I didn't tell Jacob.

He nodded slowly, like he was thinking about something that hadn't occurred to him before. "Ever notice anything strange about him?"

"Like what?" I said. I didn't think Jan was strange—until tonight at least.

"Odd phone calls? Arguments?"

"Not really." I thought about the call I'd heard last night in the hotel room. "He spoke French on the phone once."

"Anything else?"

"He had two passports," I said, wondering if I was being at all helpful. Jacob's questions seemed superfluous.

"From where?"

"Belgium and Suriname."

"Don't you think that's odd?" Jacob said.

"I guess."

"Where were you going when you decided not to go?"

"I thought Belgium," I said.

"Then what happened?"

"Jan changed his mind."

"To what?"

"He wouldn't say," I said, realizing how crazy I sounded.

Jacob let out a long sigh. It was really more of a whistle. "You're better off."

"Why?" I said, though I guess I already knew.

"I'm getting to that," he said, unbuttoning his jacket. Jacob never took his jacket off. He never stayed anywhere long enough to get comfortable. "There's good news, by the way," he said, rubbing the back of his neck. "Turns out your friend Kyle isn't our man—"

"I know," I said. It was sort of fun knowing something before Jacob told me.

"How?"

"He was at the airport."

"He's smarter than I thought," Jacob said. "Anyway . . . couple of NYU coeds," he continued, "nice girls. Art history students. Hangerman passed out at their pad the night of Christian Olsen's murder." He laughed. "They couldn't get rid of him. Spent the night there. They had the super drag his ass out."

It was sort of funny. Kyle vindicated by a couple of girls he'd probably been trying to shag.

"Super confirms," he went on.

"And the bad news?" It was obvious. But I needed to hear him say it.

Jacob stood up and made a neat circle around the room. He was slight, but his quickness made him seem bigger. "Jan—whoever he is—is our suspect now."

Jacob started tapping his notebook again. It was the only sound in the apartment.

"Why would he do it?" I said, trying to control my voice.

"You tell me."

"Tell you what? There's nothing to tell." There wasn't a logical explanation for what he was saying.

"Think about it." Jacob got up and cased the room again. "This guy Jan. He wasn't what he seemed."

"What do you mean?"

"There's no record of him," Jacob said. "Anywhere."

"I don't get it," I said, baffled.

"He doesn't exist."

"Of course he exists," I said. "I just saw him."

"His name," Jacob said. "It isn't real. He made it up."

"Not real," I repeated. I was dumbfounded.

"Yeah," Jacob said, rubbing his eyes. "I can't believe it either. But there's no record of him. Not here. Not in Belgium . . ." Jacob took a deep breath. "Did he say anything when he left?"

"Like what?" I said.

"Anything that might help us."

Jan's words came slowly back to me. "One thing . . . that didn't make sense."

"What?" In a second, Jacob was standing over me.

"He said . . . he had to save me from myself."

"Poetic," Jacob said, grimacing. "Whatever that means."

I touched the diamonds on my neck.

"Tell me one more thing," Jacob said. "Did Jan know you were sleeping with Christian?"

My face flushed. "I wasn't sleeping with Christian."

Jacob held up his hands. "Okay . . . whatever you were doing with Christian. Did Jan know?"

"I certainly didn't tell him."

"Maybe someone else did." It was more of a statement than a question. The scene with Kyle in the pool hall came back to me. Kyle had told Jan—like he said.

Jacob must've read my mind. "Christian and Jan were alone together, right?" he said.

"I'm not sure . . ." I said. "Kyle said . . ."

"Yeah," he said. "I didn't believe him either. But after the students came forward. I listened to his story again . . . it all makes sense now."

Jacob sunk into the couch and scratched his forehead. "You know, we thought it was a drug thing," he said. "And since Christian was doing some small-time dealing, that didn't seem far off. We thought Kyle knocked him off for shorting him. But that's not what went down."

I nodded slowly, trying to stay with him.

"Here's the deal," Jacob continued, clearing his throat. "Christian was receiving deliveries about once a month," he said. "This network—that's what they call it—left the dope for him at a Mail Box Plus. Then they'd call with the address where he could make the pickups. Evidently, he'd fucked up before. And they gave him a good pounding for it."

"What's this *network* thing?" I said.

"That's what Yassi Ahmet calls her expat 'friends.' Just a bunch of Algerians importing dope from the old country." Jacob rolled his eyes. "Christian must've got a call for a pickup while he was here."

I remembered the call that had taken Christian into Carmi's bedroom. "He got a call on his cell one night," I added. But Jacob seemed deep in thought.

"So Christian jots down the address for the pickup on the play—in Swedish, like a glorified piece of scrap paper. It took me a while to figure that one out. Then he carts the play back to his place. Kyle swings over on a drug buy, and takes the play for *his* reading pleasure, unaware that it's got directions on the back. Christian panics—he can't remember where the dope is. He tells Yassi, who can't get in touch with her people back home. Yassi thinks Kyle took the play to get back at her—and this is not a person you want to fuck with."

That was obvious.

"She sics her dogs on Kyle, who succeeds in getting his arms busted. Poor guy." Jacob frowned.

"That's why everyone wanted Malcolm's play," I said. It was all crystallizing.

"Yeah," Jacob said. "'Cause it led to the stash. But Kyle never noticed. He brought the play to his Off-Off Broadway theater company. From what I hear, they liked it so much, they're going to produce it." Jacob laughed. "I guess Foxman's about to be a star."

"But I thought Kyle brought the play back to Christian."

"He did," Jacob said. "But the theater director had already made a copy."

"Oh," I said, wondering if Malcolm even knew.

"So," Jacob said, "we arrested Kyle based on Jan's statement."

"Which turned out . . . ," I finished Jacob's sentence: ". . . to not be true."

Jacob didn't say anything. He didn't have to. It came to me—

all at once. Like a calculus problem you've been staring at for days. You see the logic as easily as you see your face in a mirror. I felt numb.

Jacob was still talking. "Now it's playing like a standard-issue love triangle. Very James M. Cain. Jan—whatever his name is—left Hangerman, came back here, ran into Christian, started in on him about . . . you know . . . defending his honor and that kind of nonsense." Jacob shrugged. "This Christian guy had quite the social life. Between dealing and designing, he had a lot of . . . friends. Maybe they argued and Jan hauled off and whacked him . . . Christian smacks his head and—bam!—that's the end of him." He turned his dark eyes on me.

I opened my mouth to say something. But it wasn't any use. I was officially sick, brimming with bile that was working its way up my throat.

"Jesus Christ," he said, hopping off the couch. "You're white as a sheet."

But I wasn't paying attention to him. I was in no-man's land, a place where nothing looked familiar and no one spoke my language. Jan had abandoned me there. Christian and Kyle, too. I was surrounded by liars. Jacob must've got me a glass of water because I was holding one. "We're having him picked up," he said, prodding my shoulder to make sure I was still alive. "I'll check in with you later. To see if he called."

I nodded. But I was hardly hearing him.

"I'm really sorry," Jacob said.

I heard him stomp over to the door. "Lock it behind me," he said. "And get some sleep. You look terrible." With that, he was gone.

For the first time in two months, I was alone. I went into the bathroom, leaned over the toilet, and threw up. Not much came up, a few strings of coffee water. I hadn't had dinner. I dragged myself off the floor and gargled with mouthwash. In the mirror, I was a shadow, my skin like chicken flesh. My eyes were swollen with half-moons underneath. My lips were the pinkish tone of winter tomatoes. I splashed some hot water on my face. I barely felt it. I took off the necklace and tossed it in the garbage, thinking that I'd let myself be seduced by Jan—or whoever he was. I felt betrayed, not only by Jan but by myself. Jacob's story played in my head. He'd unveiled every detail except what Christian owed Carmi. I'd have to find that out on my own. I didn't need Jacob arresting my uncle. The other thing I hadn't asked Jacob was what if I had gone with Jan? What would have become of me? I didn't even want to consider it. I didn't want to consider anything, for that matter.

I opened the medicine cabinet and nabbed the leftover sleeping pills Jan had given me. I took three and went into Carmi's bedroom. I didn't bother undressing. I threw myself on the skinny mattress and waited for the pills to work their magic. So this was what a nervous breakdown felt like. Well, it wasn't so bad. I buried my face in a pillow; I thought I could smell Jan's scent on the cotton. I'd washed everything, so I was probably imagining it. Still, I felt sick all over again.

I peeled myself off Carmi's bed and went back to the living room. If I'd had any strength, I would've gone for a walk. Instead, I flung open a window and stuck out my head. The winter air was bracing; the street looked exactly as it had on my first night. It was nice to know that at least one thing hadn't changed. I felt a little better. I was glad to be leaving. I was going back to California, getting away from here.

In the distance I could see the needle of the Empire State Building slicing through the night sky. I took in a deep breath of crisp air. It froze my lungs and made my nose run. I stayed by the window, watching the street below, watching life move on.

The pills began to kick in. I couldn't stand up any longer. I shut the window and curled up in Carmi's chair, a tattered caftan wrapped tightly around me. Soon, I nodded off into a narcotic slumber.

The shrill ring of the phone woke me up. I had no idea what time it was, but light was seeping through the curtains. Jacob was on the line. He wanted to know if I had any idea where Jan might've gone. I didn't. Jacob cursed like a madman. It seemed Jan had never technically *arrived* anywhere; his name—if that was his name—hadn't turned up on any flight. No one could recall seeing him. He'd simply disappeared. Just like he'd come and gone in my life.

Jan was on the run now, a perpetual foreigner.

chapter 35

Carmi got back around eight. He had on the same suit he'd left in, which was wrinkled now and nearly threadbare; a straw hat was still perched atop his head. Under the short brim, his face looked caramelized. When he smiled, his teeth were big and white against his smooth tan skin. He hugged me, the pleasant aroma of suntan lotion, citrus aftershave, and booze filling my nostrils. He was exhausted, a dose of Dramamine had wiped him out. "I can't tolerate turbulence, Alex," he said. "It makes me nauseous." He wanted to excuse himself until morning, and catch up over coffee. His presence made me feel at ease for the first time in days. I tried to keep him awake and talking.

I suggested a nightcap. "Maybe just one," Carmi said with a wink. I mixed a rum and Coke, which seemed appropriate, and we sat on the couch and chatted about nothing. I asked the obligatory vacation questions: Weather? Fun? Activities? Carmi was in a good mood—Puerto Rico was obviously still on his mind. But I could barely hold a conversation. The news I'd eventually have to unload weighed on me. Or maybe it was just the rum. After twenty minutes Carmi finished his drink and went to bed.

I crashed on the pull-out couch for what would be my last night in New York. Under anything like normal conditions, it would've been a sentimental moment—a final look at the evening skyline, my last chance to fall asleep to the sound of Twenty-third Street traffic. But I was still too wrapped up in the business of the past two days to wax poetic. I kept the phone close at hand; someone was bound to call. I figured Jacob would ring with more questions, or Kyle would call to brag about surviving his latest brush with the law. I didn't want them waking up Carmi before I had a chance to explain. I was even half-expecting Jan to call from God knows where. I laid there with my eyes open and my mind humming.

I looked at my watch. It was only ten thirty—no wonder I wasn't tired. I tried to read but couldn't concentrate. My mind kept drifting back to Jan. Even if what Jacob said about him was true, I couldn't help but think about him. I didn't know what that said about me. Maybe I *had* been in love with him. It was hard to believe he'd actually killed someone. He'd always seemed so collected, so gentle. But I guess you never really knew what someone was capable of.

I imagined Jan on a white sandy beach somewhere, the Indian Ocean lapping his toes. Or maybe he'd hidden himself in a rain forest in Indonesia. Anything seemed possible. One day I might run into him in a crowded market in the Caribbean, or a smoky opium den in Amsterdam. I hoped I would. I wanted the chance to ask him why he'd done it.

I'd been duped. That was the worst realization. Worse than anything else that had happened since Christian died. I'd misjudged. I'd been dead wrong about all of them: Kyle, Christian, and Jan. It was as though I'd lost my balance and taken a bad fall down a flight of stairs. All that was missing was the broken hip and bruises.

The phone woke me, as I knew it would, at three o'clock in the morning. "Hello?" I whispered. "Jan?" I was sure it was him. I could feel it. But there was no answer. Just the dull static of a broken television. I thought I heard Arabic in the background, but I was probably imagining it. An hour later, the phone rang again. This time, I was ready. I picked it up. "Jan?" I said, waiting to hear his voice.

"It's me."

"Who me?"

"Kyle. Who the fuck else?"

As though he were the only person in the world.

"Hi," I said.

"What's up?"

"It's *four* o'clock in the morning."

"I know," he said.

"Then why are you calling me?"

"I wanted to make sure you didn't leave."

"I didn't," I said.

"I thought you might."

"I'm still here."

"Obviously," he said.

"What are you doing?"

"I couldn't sleep," he coughed a little. "This fuckin' arm . . . it itches."

Kyle's logic: I can't sleep, so neither should anyone else.

"You're leaving soon, right?"

I didn't say anything. He was being rhetorical.

"I was thinking," he continued. "Maybe I ought to skip this dump of a town with you. I'm sick of it." He yawned. "My luck isn't so good here."

As though his luck had ever been good anywhere. Still, I could hear a tiny bit of repentance in his voice. If he was leaving, maybe we could hit the road together.

"I leave tomorrow," I said. "At eight."

There was a long silence.

"They say he did it."

"I know," I said.

"Did they get him?"

"No," I said. "He didn't go back to Belgium. He just . . . vanished."

"I knew he was fucked up."

"You were right," I said. I had to admit it.

"See?"

"See what?"

"Sometimes I know what I'm doin'."

"I'll keep it in mind," I said.

"But you can't help yourself." He laughed. "You've always had fucked-up taste in men."

It may have been the most perceptive moment of Kyle's life. There wasn't anything left to say.

"So, I'll see you tomorrow?" he said.

"I guess."

"Later."

The phone went dead.

The next night, Kyle turned up just as they were about to shut the airplane door. When he saw me, he grinned. And I have to admit, I had an ear-to-ear smile across my face, too. His arm was still bent up in a cast, but he had on new clothes and his hair was neatly plastered to his head. He looked like Dennis the Menace. Maybe he'd turned over a new leaf—if only for the moment. I was genuinely glad to see him, though I couldn't really say why. He probably felt the same way; he'd brought me a couple of books he thought I'd like. That was about all you could ask for from Kyle. His small gestures were like giant ones from someone else. So we flew back together, sitting side-by-side like long-lost friends. Kyle was making me forget what had happened in New York by talking about San Francisco. The closer we got to California the better I felt. In fact, by the time I saw the Grand Canyon thirty thousand feet below us, I was myself all over again. Well, almost.

• • •

Before my flight, Carmi had taken me out to a neighborhood Greek restaurant for an early dinner. I'd managed to make it through half the day without mentioning the activities in the apartment next door. Somehow, the various building staff—doormen, repairmen, super, and so on—hadn't gotten to him yet either. I'd have to be the one to break the news. My bags were packed. A car had been arranged. I'd heard from Jacob; he wanted my number in California. Did I ever "accept" visitors from the East Coast? He was thinking about a transfer. New York was too cold for him. And by the way, did I know Robinson Jeffers's house in Carmel? He'd once been asked to read one of his poems to a bunch of tourists. Maybe we'd go there? His anecdote intrigued me—a cop who liked poetry. I said I was trying not to entertain out-of-town guests, but in his case, I'd make an exception. We'd left it at that.

My uncle was back to his old self, glum as ever. We had taken a table at the back. Carmi never sat near the door: "It's the place most people get pickpocketed," he assured me. He'd ordered a jug of retsina and a bunch of appetizers from a waiter with a wandering eye before I had a chance to look at the menu. That was fine. Carmi evidently came here a lot; he knew what he liked. There were nautical paintings and nets on the walls. A folktune poured from a speaker in the corner. The place was empty. It was only five.

The waiter returned with the retsina. "I wonder, dear," Carmi said, filling our glasses. "Did you ever see Christian?"

I wished Carmi hadn't brought it up so soon; I wanted to tell him later so I wouldn't spoil our dinner. I decided it could wait a little longer. "A couple of times," I said. It was still so strange talking about Christian as if he were alive, wandering around somewhere. I liked to imagine he was.

the foreigner_____**MEG CASTALDO**

"Well," Carmi said, taking a swig. "You'll never believe this . . ."

I'd braced myself for another weird tale.

". . . That Christian took two thousand dollars from me." He gulped his retsina.

"For what?"

"A down payment," he said. "For my plans."

"Your plans?"

Carmi nodded. "I paid him," Carmi said. "But he never delivered."

"I'm sorry," I said, not really knowing why I was apologizing for Christian. "What plans?"

"For my new kitchen." Carmi chuckled. "Didn't you see the paint swatches in the kitchen? He wanted to expand my palette."

I had seen them, but I'd never connected the two . . .

"I'll tell you, Alex, I wasn't wild about his ideas, but he was so pushy." He drained his glass.

It was nice to know that Christian had been consistent in every area of his life.

"What did you think I was talking about, dear?" Carmi asked.

"Never mind," I said, sighing.

So that explained that. It turned out that Carmi had been worried about his two thousand dollars. Who could blame him? I didn't have the strength to tell him he'd never get it back. A waiter brought out a tray of small plates heaped with roasted peppers, squid, tzatziki, stuffed grape leaves, olives, and so on. It reeked of garlic. We dug in, not speaking for a while. Then Carmi said: "You know, Alex, Puerto Rico is a liberal place."

"Is that so?" I'd said.

He nodded. "People there . . ." He popped an olive in his mouth. "They understand that everyone is different."

"That's good," I said, wondering what he was getting at now.

"You can learn a lot in an atmosphere like that."

"I'm sure you can."

He paused to wave at a portly guy in a gray sharkskin suit who was probably the owner.

"So, Carmi," I said, "tell me what you did in Puerto Rico."

"Well," Carmi said, "I saw an old friend."

"That must've been nice," I said, nodding a bit too earnestly.

Carmi took a bite of squid and made a face. "This tastes like it came out of the Hudson," he said, pushing the plate away. Then he picked up his train of thought. "I've known Julio for years."

I didn't say anything. It seemed like he was about to launch into a lengthy vacation anecdote. I leaned back in my chair. But he only said: "Julio is very dear to me."

My face must've looked surprisingly naive to Carmi because what he said next nearly made me laugh with embarrassment. He paused, his fork poised above a plate of beef patties, and added: "You know, Alex, boys don't just like girls . . . and girls just don't like boys." He smiled as though he was filling me in on a great cosmic secret. Then he stabbed a disk of meat and shook it onto his plate. I didn't say anything. He'd said it all.

"The beef is excellent," Carmi said, chewing slowly. He turned his green eyes on me. "So, Alex, tell me what went on in New York while I was away?"

I took a deep breath. "Well, Carmi," I said, "you'll never believe what happened. It all started the day you left . . ."

And I told him.

Epilogue

Two years later, I stumbled on a poster in Berkeley with Yassi's picture printed on it. I was sure it was her, even though the poster said her name was Issay. She was part of a symposium on feminism. Her topic was Jane Austen: The First Modern Woman. I thought about checking it out just to see Yassi's latest incarnation. When I told Jacob about it, he said I was mistaken. As far as he knew, Yassi was back in Algeria. But I suspected he was wrong.

After a few months in San Francisco, Kyle got bored and moved to Atlanta. He was recruited by the World Wrestling Federation. His ring name is Heat Miser. He's currently undefeated. As for me, I'm in my second year of law school. Jacob lives with me; we study criminal law together.

Malcolm lives in Hollywood. Once in a while he sends me a postcard.

Carmi still hasn't redone his kitchen.

Acknowledgments

Thanks to Jessica Green for her generous wisdom; Joe Olshan and Barry Raine for their confidence and commiseration; Mitria DiGiacomo and Dorothy Cavyn-Pege for believing; Angie Eng for understanding; Jason Anderson for existing; Bruce Diones, Michael Hainey, Silvana Nova, and Craig Seligman for always asking; Richard Abate for keeping the faith; Greer Kessel Hendricks for her enthusiasm; Roberta Rosenberg and Bob Cavagna for a place to escape; and, of course, to my parents for putting up with me, and the entire Castaldo clan for always keeping things interesting.

Acknowledgments

Like this is the only one...

Floating
Robin Troy

The Perks of Being a Wallflower
Stephen Chbosky

The Fuck-up
Arthur Nersesian

Dreamworld
Jane Goldman

Fake Liar Cheat
Tod Goldberg

Pieces
edited by Stephen Chbosky

Dogrun
Arthur Nersesian

Brave New Girl
Louisa Luna

More from the young, the hip,
and the up-and-coming.
Brought to you by MTV Books.

POCKET
BOOKS